P9-AZW-360

Praise for
A Wreath of Snow

"I loved it. *A Wreath of Snow* is a wonderful story of redemption and restoration that will warm your heart during the Christmas season—or any time of year!"

—FRANCINE RIVERS, author of *Redeeming Love*

"When *A Wreath of Snow* arrived at my doorstep, I settled down to read just a few lines and instead devoured it. I highly recommend this book to anyone who enjoys heart-tugging stories of forgiveness and grace."

—TRACIE PETERSON, author of the Land of the Lone Star series

"A delightful Christmas jaunt through bonny Scotland in the Victorian era—complete with snow! I was drawn in by compelling characters who struggle to find love, joy, and belonging, only to discover the real meaning of Christmas. A heartwarming story!"

—MELODY CARLSON, author of *Christmas at Harrington's*

"*A Wreath of Snow* charms from first page to last, and Gordon and Meg will capture your heart. The story might even make you long for snow. Don't miss this delightful novella. It's a keeper!"

—ROBIN LEE HATCHER, author of *Betrayal*

"Journey to a time and place where hearth, home, and honesty are the gifts beneath the candlelit Christmas tree. You'll find yourself lingering in the glow of this winsome tale that brims with comfort and joy."

—Robin Jones Gunn, author of *Finding Father Christmas*

"I look for a richly textured story that draws me in and lets me become a part of its world. Liz Curtis Higgs has once again provided that kind of beautifully written and thoroughly involving story. *A Wreath of Snow* glows with warmth, charm, and grace. A wonderful read."

—BJ Hoff, author of The Riverhaven Years series

"Like a perfect afternoon tea, *A Wreath of Snow* is sure to comfort, delight, and surprise. It offers the savory rewards of repentance tendered and forgiveness received, the liquid warmth of family affections, and a perfectly delicate setting in Victorian Scotland. A charming Christmas read."

—Sandra Byrd, author of *To Die For: A Novel of Anne Boleyn*

Praise for
Mine Is the Night

"When a beautifully written, well-researched romance filled with intelligent, complicated characters comes along, it is definitely cause for celebration."

—Crosswalk.com

A
WREATH
of
SNOW

Other Books by Liz Curtis Higgs

Historical Fiction

Thorn in My Heart

Fair Is the Rose

Whence Came a Prince

Grace in Thine Eyes

Here Burns My Candle

Mine Is the Night

Contemporary Fiction

Mixed Signals

Bookends

Nonfiction

Bad Girls of the Bible

Really Bad Girls of the Bible

Unveiling Mary Magdalene

Slightly Bad Girls of the Bible

Rise and Shine

Embrace Grace

My Heart's in the Lowlands

The Girl's Still Got It

Children's

The Parable of the Lily

The Sunflower Parable

The Pumpkin Patch Parable

The Pine Tree Parable

Go Away, Dark Night

A WREATH
of
SNOW

A Victorian Christmas Novella

LIZ CURTIS HIGGS

WaterBrook
PRESS

A Wreath of Snow

All Scripture quotations are taken from the King James Version.

The characters and events in this book are fictional, and any resemblance to actual persons or events is coincidental.

Hardcover ISBN 978-1-4000-7217-0
eBook ISBN 978-0-307-72956-9

Copyright © 2012 by Liz Curtis Higgs

Cover design by Mark D. Ford; cover photo of woman by Laurence Dutton, Getty Images

All rights reserved. No part of this book may be reproduced or transmitted in any form or by any means, electronic or mechanical, including photocopying and recording, or by any information storage and retrieval system, without permission in writing from the publisher.

Published in the United States by WaterBrook, an imprint of the Crown Publishing Group, a division of Penguin Random House LLC, New York.

WaterBrook® and its deer colophon are registered trademarks of Penguin Random House LLC.

Library of Congress Cataloging-in-Publication Data
Higgs, Liz Curtis.
    A wreath of snow / Liz Curtis Higgs. — 1st ed.
        p. cm.
    ISBN 978-1-4000-7217-0 (alk. paper) — ISBN 978-0-307-72956-9 (electronic)
    1. Scotland—Social life and customs—19th century—Fiction. I. Title.
    PS3558.I36235W48 2005
    813'.54—dc23

                                        2012028073

Printed in the United States of America
2018

10 9 8 7 6

To our daughter, Lilly,
a brilliant artist, a gifted storyteller,
a fine traveling companion,
and an exceptional encourager

Christmas...
the season for kindling, not merely
the fire of hospitality in the hall,
but the genial flame of charity
in the heart.

WASHINGTON IRVING

Chapter One

Christmas is here:
Winds whistle shrill,
Icy and chill.

WILLIAM MAKEPEACE THACKERAY

Stirling, Scotland
24 December 1894

In all her twenty-six years, Meg Campbell had never been this cold. Shivering inside her green woolen coat, she passed the crowded shops of Murray Place as the snow fell thick and fast.

She could only guess when the next train would depart for Edinburgh. Why had she not consulted her father's railway schedule posted by the kitchen door? Because she left

Albert Place in tears. Because she left without even saying good-bye.

Meg lowered her chin lest a gust of wind catch the brim of her hat and wrench it from her head. Another minute and she would reach the corner. Two minutes more and—

"Mind where you're going, lass!"

Startled, she nearly lost her balance on the icy pavement. "Beg pardon, Mr. Fenwick."

Her former schoolteacher, now bent with age, merely grunted in response.

"I'm Margaret Campbell," she reminded him, knowing how many students had passed through his classroom door. "Have you heard that I'm a teacher now? In Edinburgh?"

"Aye." He stared at her for a moment, then tottered off without another word, the tip of his cane drawing a jagged pattern in the snow.

Meg turned away, slightly stung by the elderly man's rebuff. Perhaps Mr. Fenwick believed unmarried women should reside at home with their families. If so, he was not alone in his opinion. But he didn't know what life was like beneath her parents' roof. *I tried to stay, Mum. Truly I did.*

Gripping her leather satchel, Meg headed toward Station Road, glancing at the shop windows with their mounds of fresh oranges and brightly colored paper bells. Her two dozen students would be home by now, celebrating Christmas with their loved ones. Just picturing bright-eyed Eliza Grant holding up her chalk slate covered with numbers and Jamie McFarlane shouting out the alphabet with glee renewed Meg's confidence. She was living in the right place and doing the work she was called to do, no matter what the Mr. Fenwicks of the world might think.

The heavy snowfall muted the clatter of horses' hoofs in the busy thoroughfare and washed every bit of color from the sky. Was it two o'clock? Three? She'd been so upset when she left her parents' house that she hadn't checked the watch pinned to her bodice or arranged for a carriage. Now she had to send for her trunk and hope it could be delivered to the railway station in time for her departure.

She turned the corner and was relieved to see a host of arriving passengers pouring into the street. It seemed the trains were running despite the weather. Easing her pace to manage the downward slope, Meg held out one hand, prepared to grasp a hitching post—or a stranger's elbow, if need be.

Few pedestrians were moving in the direction she was. Instead, they were flowing upward into the town. Gentlemen returning home from the city, cousins gathering for Christmas, young scholars toting ice skates instead of books—all were tramping up snowy Station Road with joy on their faces.

Guilt, as sharp as the wintry wind, swept over Meg. Her parents had looked anything but joyful when she'd quit Albert

Place. Her brother, Alan, was the reason she'd left, yet Meg had hurt her father and mother all the same. "Forgive me," she whispered, wishing she'd said those words earlier.

For two long years she'd avoided a visit home, praying time might dislodge the bitterness that had taken root in her brother's heart. But when she'd arrived in Stirling last evening, she'd discovered the sad truth. Alan Campbell, four years her junior, was even more churlish and demanding than she'd remembered and greedy as well, a new and unwelcome affliction.

His parting words would follow her back to Edinburgh—to Thistle Street, to Aunt Jean's house, to *her* house. "What a selfish creature you are, Meg." She flinched even now, remembering the cruel look on her brother's face and the sharpness of his tone. "You could have sold the house Aunt Jean gave you and shared the earnings with your family."

You mean with you, Alan.

Meg lifted the hem of her coat and stepped with care through the slush and dirt the horse-drawn carriages left behind. She could hardly deny Alan's needs were greater than her own. But when she'd moved to Edinburgh to care for their late aunt, wrapping her aching limbs with compresses and feeding her bowls of hot soup, Meg had never imagined Aunt Jean would choose to bless her only niece with the gift of her town house.

"Father should have been her heir," Alan had insisted. Aunt Jean's will, written in her neat hand, stated otherwise.

Over the midday meal Meg's conversation with her brother had deteriorated into thinly veiled accusations on his part and tearful denials on hers, until she could bear no more. To be treated so unkindly, and on Christmas Eve! Her parents had tried to intervene, but Alan's temper was not easily managed. Their patience with him was a testimony to their Christian charity. And to their love, though Meg wondered if guilt did not play an equal role.

Meg wove through the crowd and kept her head down lest someone recognize her and draw her into a discussion. Much as it grieved her, she had no polite banter to offer, no cheerful holiday sentiments. By tomorrow her mood would surely brighten. Just now she wished to tend her wounds in private.

She stepped across the threshold into the railway station and brushed off the snow that clung to her coat, glad to be out of the wind. Inside the nearby booking office a cast-iron stove glowed with heat, steaming up the windows. But in the waiting area and across the broad, open platform, winter prevailed. Holly wreaths, their crimson berries bright against the dark green leaves, decorated the painted iron pillars supporting the roof. Everyone's arms were filled with packages, as if Saint Nicholas had already come and gone.

Meg glanced at the clock mounted below the arched ceiling, then scanned the departure times posted for the Caledonian Railway. The southbound line, which stopped at Larbert, Falkirk, and Linlithgow en route to Edinburgh, departed at three twenty-six. Little more than an hour remained to collect her baggage.

When a middle-aged porter lumbered past, bearing a trunk far larger than her own, Meg hurried after him. "Sir, might I engage your services?" As he swung around with an expectant look on his face, she paused, her resolve flagging. How might her family respond when a porter asked for her belongings? Her mother would surely burst into tears. And her brother? He would probably want the contents of her trunk tossed into the street.

Determined not to lose heart, Meg reached for the small coin purse inside her satchel. "I've a single trunk to be transported from Albert Place onto the next train bound for Edinburgh," she told the porter. She then informed him of the address and offered enough silver to guarantee his cooperation.

"I know the house, miss." The coins disappeared into his pocket. "Soon as I deliver this trunk, I'll see to yours."

She sent him on his way, glancing up at the clock, hoping he would catch her meaning. *Hurry, hurry.*

The queue at the booking window was blessedly short. Before she could join the handful of outbound travelers waiting to purchase tickets, a small dog appeared and began nipping at the hem of her coat. "Aren't you a fine wee pup?" she murmured, bending down to stroke the young terrier. Even through her gloves she could feel his wiry coat and the light nip of his teeth as he playfully turned his head this way and that.

Above the din floated a high, reedy voice. "Can it be Miss Campbell come back at last?"

Edith Darroch. Of all the gossips in Stirling, she took the prize.

Meg slowly rose to face the woman, who served up savory news and idle rumors like a hostess offering scones and jam. Though Edith's hair had faded to the color of ashes, her eyes were bright with interest.

"Mrs. Darroch," Meg said, "are you bound for Alloa to spend Christmas with your son?"

"Indeed not." The older woman gave her terrier's leash a swift tug. "Johnny is returning home for the holidays, as any loving child should do. I expect him on the next train." After a cursory glance about the station, she asked, "Is your family not here to greet you?"

The question pierced Meg's heart. Her parents had met her train last evening. But on this bitterly cold afternoon, she was very much on her own.

"I suppose your brother cannot brave such weather," Mrs. Darroch continued, her voice oozing sympathy. "It would be a shame if he injured himself further."

"He didn't injure himself," Meg said firmly, rising to her brother's defense. However strained their relationship, Alan was her only sibling. "Gordon Shaw struck him with a curling stone." Hadn't Meg stood beside the pond at King's Park that January afternoon a dozen years ago and watched in horror as a red-headed young man with whisky on his breath heaved a forty-pound curling stone through the air?

The damage to Alan's lower back was invisible to the eye, but Meg could not ignore the pained expression on her brother's face whenever he struggled to his feet, leaning hard on their father's arm. He'd had a difficult young life, to be sure. And he'd made their parents' lives difficult as well, not just because of his injury, but also because of his irritable nature, which their father and mother seemed unwilling or unable to curb.

"A tragedy," Mrs. Darroch agreed and took a breath as if preparing for a lengthy discourse on the subject.

"Next customer, please," the booking clerk called out.

Grateful for a swift end to any further discussion of Alan, Meg turned to find the queue empty and the clerk waving her forward. She hurried to the window, then leaned in to murmur her request, hoping Mrs. Darroch was out of earshot.

A pointless gesture, Meg realized. The woman would learn

of her hasty departure soon enough. So would their many neighbors on Albert Place. Meg could almost hear them now from a quarter mile away.

That Campbell woman wasn't home a day.

Aye, and left before Christmas.

You can be sure she broke her mother's heart.

It's not the first time nor likely the last. Poor Lorna Campbell.

Meg fished out two more silver coins, swallowing the lump in her throat. Why had she not sent a note with the porter? She would write to her mother at once—on the train if she could keep her hand steady enough to form the words. *I am sorry, Mum. So very sorry.* Meg would also gently remind her parents that Edinburgh was her home now and only an hour away by rail. *Come visit me, Mum. Soon.*

The booking clerk, an amiable fellow with wavy hair and a slender mustache, gently pressed the ticket into her hand. "You'll be wanting your tea." He pointed toward a wooden counter facing the platform where passengers stood huddled about, cups and saucers in hand. "Ha'penny a cup."

Her spirits somewhat buoyed at the prospect of a hot drink, Meg took a circuitous route to avoid Mrs. Darroch, who was busy scolding her puppy. No doubt the train pulling into the station numbered Johnny Darroch among its passengers. Wrapped in a cloud of steam, the engine rolled to a stop, the screech of metal against metal filling the frosty air.

Meg paused at the bookstall next to platform three, thinking a novel might offer a welcome distraction. She quickly made a selection, then approached the rosy-cheeked cashier dispensing tea and coffee. A whirl of snow blew across the railway platform and around Meg's calfskin walking boots. The weather definitely was not improving. Some Decembers in Stirling were snowy, others merely cold. The winter she had turned fifteen, they'd had flakes the size of shillings and had measured the snow in feet.

She ordered tea with milk and sugar, eying the currant buns and sweet mincemeat tarts displayed beneath a bell jar. Later, perhaps, when her appetite returned. At the moment, her stomach was twisted into a knot.

"Anything else for you?" the cashier asked as she handed over the tea, steaming and fragrant.

Meg was surprised to find her fingers trembling when she lifted the cup. "All I want is a safe journey home."

"On a day like this?" the round-faced woman exclaimed. "None but the Almighty can promise you that, lass."

Chapter Two

I've that within—
for which there are no plasters!

DAVID GARRICK

Gordon Shaw stood at the far end of the railway platform beyond the roof, his footprints hidden under a fresh layer of snow. He grimaced at the irony. *Covering your tracks, eh?*

No one had noticed him slip into Stirling early that morning, as dark as it was. He'd exited the train, pulled his tweed cap low over his brow, and walked with purpose to Dumbarton Road.

Even after twelve years, Stirling was quite as he'd remembered: an overcrowded hill town filled with endless regrets.

He'd not wanted to return, not even for one day. But what could he tell his newspaper editor without raising suspicion? Best to do the work and keep his wretched past to himself.

By noon he'd finished his assignment and had stuffed a sheaf of notes into his traveling bag. Last Thursday a photographer from the *Glasgow Herald* had captured a fair likeness of his interview subject. Nothing remained but writing the article itself. That could be easily handled once he arrived in Edinburgh, where another interview awaited him after Boxing Day.

"Surely you'll not spend Christmas at the Waterloo Hotel," his editor had said with an incredulous look on his face.

Gordon had shrugged, pretending not to mind. "Clean sheets, hot meals. As good as home, though don't tell Mrs. Wilson I said so." His housekeeper tidied his four rooms each weekday afternoon, then left a warm supper for him in the oven and the table set for one. He usually read the *Scotsman* while he dined, too absorbed with the rival newspaper to dwell on how quiet it was in his parlor.

As for the holidays, they were best spent elsewhere, keeping his mind off all that he'd lost and could not regain. In his lodging house he was surrounded by furnishings that had once belonged to his parents—the oak sideboard, the brass and copper table lamps, the blue-and-white china lining the picture rail, the upholstered sofa with its rich fabric and deep buttoning, the corner whatnots with their many shelves. Though he'd not spent a penny of his inheritance, Gordon was grateful to use the household goods he'd known so well. On most days they were a comfort to him. But not at Christmastide.

Last December he'd found an excuse to head for Dumfries. This year it was Stirling, then Edinburgh. Leaving Glasgow for a few days provided another benefit: Mrs. Wilson would celebrate the Lord's birth with her family rather than fret over him.

He peered down the tracks, listening intently, his gloved hands fisted inside his coat pockets, the *Stirling Observer* tucked under one arm. Though the southbound train was due any moment, the heavy snow made it difficult to tell if the engine was approaching. As other passengers began moving onto the platform, he turned his back toward them and hunched his shoulders closer to his ears, willing the train to arrive before someone recognized him.

It was not likely he'd be discovered, Gordon reminded himself. He'd left Stirling a smooth-faced lad of seventeen with lanky forearms poking out of his too-short sleeves. Now he sported a closely trimmed beard even redder than the hair on his head and a wool suit tailored to his fuller, taller frame. Time had done its duty by him. Once he reached Edinburgh, any fear of being identified could be put to rest.

His conscience prodded him. *Is that all that matters, Shaw? Your reputation? What about the injured lad? What about Alan Campbell?*

Gordon shifted his stance, uncomfortable with such questions. Of course the Campbell boy mattered. He would be a man now. Twenty-two. Bedridden, perhaps, his legs all but useless.

Every detail of that January afternoon was seared into Gordon's memory, from the fir trees beside the curling pond at King's Park to the frigid weather, even colder than today. It seemed all of Stirlingshire had gathered along the edge of the pond, waiting for the match to begin, when he stumbled onto the ice, laughing and loose-limbed from too many drams of whisky. He grabbed his curling stone by the handle and swept the heavy, teapot-shaped stone around him in a lopsided circle, taunting the other lads by promising to crown one of them King of the Bean for Twelfth Night.

Then it happened. Gordon lost his grip on the handle just as ten-year-old Alan Campbell darted onto the ice. The granite curling stone struck the lad squarely in the lower back. Alan cried out in such pain that every spectator turned to see who was injured. And who was responsible.

I didn't mean to hurt him.

How many times had Gordon said those words? Though his apology that night was sincere, it could not heal the little boy or comfort the sister who held him across her lap, weeping.

The town turned against him overnight. When he knocked on the Campbells' door to apologize, he was not received.

When he wrote to the family, the letters were returned un-opened. Within weeks he left Stirling in disgrace to seek a fresh start in Glasgow. His parents had remained in Stirling until they could bear the shame no longer and moved south to Eng-land, his mother's home.

Since that January afternoon Gordon hadn't touched a drop of whisky, hadn't missed a Sunday in church, hadn't given any man or woman further cause to despise him. He'd also re-fused to touch a curling stone, praying the Lord would heal Alan and undo the damage his carelessness had wrought. But here in the town of his birth, memories ran deep, and forgive-ness was hard to come by.

In the distance a shrill whistle pierced the air. Gordon eased closer to the rails, anxious to be gone from Stirling, to disappear like the Ochil Hills that were now hidden behind a thickening curtain of snow. When the train finally entered the station and ground to a halt, he bolted through one of the narrow wooden doors, then headed toward two vacant seats at the front of a second-class carriage. He chose the spot by the window and placed his bag beside him, hoping no one would have need of the aisle seat.

Seeking refuge behind his newspaper, Gordon scanned the columns of ink. The choppy cadence of the voices around him marked them as Stirling men. "Sons of the Rock," they were called, a nod to the massive crag that dominates the town, with old Stirling Castle at its pinnacle. As a lad he'd chased many a ball down Castle Wynd. Some of the men conversing behind him had probably done the same. He might even find fellow curlers among them. Old friends who'd long forgotten him. Or who remembered him all too well.

Gordon looked over his shoulder. Was the dark-haired fellow one of the Gillespie brothers? Hard to be certain. Stuart and Roy would both be in their thirties now. He eyed the other travelers, recognizing none of them. Not the older man clenching his unlit pipe between his teeth or the surly lad with a jagged scar across his chin or the small woman bearing a rambunctious toddler in her arms.

He was about to face forward again when a burst of icy air heralded another passenger's arrival. A young woman wearing a large black hat hastened through the carriage, her expression troubled. She claimed the seat across the aisle from him, placed a small satchel at her feet, then folded her hands in her lap. Her movements were efficient, her posture straight as a plumb line.

Gordon regarded her out of the corner of his eye. Most Scotswomen of his acquaintance had dark or coppery hair and freckled skin, but this one was fair-haired with a porcelain complexion. Not a woman he'd likely forget if he ever had the good fortune of being introduced. Was she a Stirling lass?

When she glanced at him from beneath the brim of her

hat, Gordon noted the hint of sorrow in her clear blue eyes. Perhaps she was bound for a funeral. A sad thought, especially on Christmas Eve.

He returned to his *Stirling Observer,* but the printed words blurred as his mind wandered back in her direction. Something about her seemed vaguely familiar. Had their paths crossed before? In a restaurant, perhaps? A theatre lobby? Her bright eyes suggested an equally bright mind. If she was from Glasgow, he might have seen her at a lecture or noticed her across a shelf of library books at the university. Gordon ventured a sidelong glance, then waited for her to look his way again.

After a bit she raised her chin to meet his gaze once more. Though he saw no spark of recognition in her eyes, he did note a slight flicker of interest. Or was he imagining that too?

When she looked away, Gordon reluctantly did the same, then folded his newspaper, weary of the pretense. Without a proper introduction he could not engage her in conversation, much as he might wish to. Little remained but to stare out the window, willing the snow to stop and the train to move.

A long ten minutes crawled by, then twenty, then forty. Consulting his pocket watch did not improve things. He looked at the wind forming snowdrifts—*wreaths,* his Scottish granny had called them—against the base of the platform and over the wheels of the train. They had no hills to climb en route to

Edinburgh and only a minor curve in the track before Falkirk station. Was it not better to press on rather than wait for even more snow to accumulate?

When the railway conductor stepped into the back of the carriage, the passengers turned to him as one, seeking answers.

"You'll be wanting to know what's delayed our departure," the conductor said matter-of-factly, his broad face chapped from the wind. "Ice on the tracks. The wheels cannot get any purchase. We've sent men ahead to clear the way, but…" He shook his head. "Could be six o'clock. Could be later."

Gordon didn't like the sound of that. How much later?

"Disembark if you wish." The conductor gestured toward the platform, dusting the nearby passengers with snow from his coat sleeve. "Spend the night in Stirling."

Impossible. Gordon nearly said the word aloud.

The fair-haired woman across from him looked distraught as well. "Will you not keep trying, Mr. McGregor?"

"Aye," the conductor assured her, "for we've passengers at each station down the line waiting for our arrival. You're welcome to stay on board. As long as the ashpan doesn't become caked with snow, we'll have enough draught to keep the coal burning and the carriages warm."

Gordon glanced out the window at a sky now the color of ink. Nightfall came early in December, swiftly dropping the temperature.

The conductor moved toward the door. "The weather may yet improve, Miss Campbell."

Campbell? Gordon was taken aback, though her surname was common enough. Campbells resided in every corner of Scotland.

"Then I shall wait," she replied, turning forward in her seat.

Gordon didn't move, riveted to her silhouette. That small upturned nose. That determined tilt to her chin. Why had he not noticed such details earlier?

Her mouth was not shaped in an anguished O, nor were her blue eyes filled with tears as they had been on the curling pond twelve winters past. But Gordon had no doubt of her identity.

The young woman seated across from him was Alan Campbell's sister.

Chapter Three

Snow had fallen, snow on snow,
snow on snow,
In the bleak midwinter, long ago.

CHRISTINA ROSSETTI

M eg clasped her hands so tightly her fingers ached. *Spend the night in Stirling?* She could only imagine what her brother would say if she reappeared on Albert Place. Whatever the hour, whatever the weather, the train had to reach Edinburgh tonight.

While many of the passengers collected their luggage and abandoned their seats, Meg smoothed her plaid wool scarf around her neck and settled in for the duration. She tried not to think about the mincemeat tarts at Stirling station. At least she'd had a cup of tea. And in one of her coat pockets was an apple that had traveled with her yesterday. She might be grateful for it by journey's end.

The second-class carriage grew decidedly quieter. Colder too. Beyond the slender glass windows, the wind howled down the tracks, pushing the snow like a plough. Only the mother with her small child remained aboard, along with the attractive bearded gentleman sitting across from Meg.

When they'd exchanged glances earlier, Meg thought she'd noted a hint of interest on his part, so she'd responded in kind. But now he was merely staring at her, a look of distress on his face.

When she could bear it no longer, Meg asked, "Is something wrong, sir?"

He straightened at once, a tinge of red rising above his collar. "No, miss. I beg your pardon." With a dutiful lift of his cap, he turned away.

Meg sank back against the seat, wishing her tone had been gentler. Instead, she'd sounded like the teacher she was, questioning him as if he were a disruptive student.

No wonder men kept their distance! Hadn't they always, even before she went to university? Over the years her quick tongue and independent spirit had driven away the few suitors who'd knocked on her door. Most of the time she'd been relieved, but once or twice she'd been very sorry indeed.

Inside the chest of drawers in her bedroom on Albert Place was a scarf she'd knitted years ago for a promising fellow named Peter Forsyth. After they'd walked out together several Sundays in a row, she'd made the handsome blue scarf for him, convinced they would be engaged by Martinmas. Later that autumn, when Mr. Forsyth stopped calling, the woolen scarf was hidden away, along with her disappointment.

Then there was Mr. Wallace, who'd grown weary of her correcting his grammar and told her so. And Mr. Alexander, who'd briefly courted her until she admitted her fondness for tidy desks and freshly sharpened pencils. And provincial Mr. Duff, whose ardor waned when she confessed her longing to explore the world beyond Stirlingshire.

If this red-haired gentleman's interest in her was genuine, Meg feared she'd already put a stopper in it. Would she never learn?

Meg sighed, then unbuttoned her coat long enough to consult the round silver watch pinned to her bodice. *Four thirty.* If Mr. McGregor was right, it could be more than an hour before they were under way. Only then did she remember the book she'd purchased at the station—*The Master of Ballantrae,* a slim, clothbound volume by the late Mr. Stevenson. Meg reached into her coat pocket to retrieve it, glad for the company of a story.

But even Lord Durrisdeer's century-old secret couldn't hold her attention on such a night. After a few pages she slipped the novel into her satchel. Too much weighed on her heart—the endless snow, the uncertain delay, and most of all the painful conversation with her brother. *Grievous words stir up anger.* However long ago Meg had learned that proverb, she'd witnessed the truth of it this day.

She shifted in her seat, trying to find the last bit of heat in the metal foot warmer, stocked earlier with coals from the locomotive's firebox. Soon enough she would be safe and warm in her Thistle Street house with her fireplace glowing and a teakettle whistling on the stove.

On her walk home from the Princes Street station, candles would be burning in nearly every window, and rich, crisp shortbread would be baking in countless ovens. She'd not left much in her larder, thinking to be gone for a full week. But she had enough butter, sugar, and flour for one circle of shortbread notched around the edges like yule cakes of old.

At the moment, however, the weather was foremost in her mind. Hours into the storm, the snow had turned into a sharp, fine dust, like ground glass, whipping past the windows of the train. A sense of foreboding washed over her. What if the signal posts became frozen and two trains were inadvertently directed onto the same track? It had happened before, on the Great Northern Railway. Or what if the ashpan became caked with snow, and the engine stopped, leaving them stranded in the countryside without heat?

Go home. Her heartbeat quickened at the strong and unexpected urging.

Home to Edinburgh? Or home to Albert Place?

She eyed the carriage door. A handful of people were still milling about the platform. Might the same porter reclaim her trunk? Arrange for it to be delivered to her parents' house and her with it? Meg knew the answer. Not in this weather, not for any amount of silver. Nor was she prepared to face her brother and hear yet again all the ways she'd disappointed him.

To Edinburgh, then.

As if at her bidding, the train whistle blew loud and long. Then the engine jolted forward with a great burst of steam. Though two hours behind schedule, the three twenty-six was finally under way.

Relieved, Meg glanced back at the woman traveling with her child, thinking to exchange smiles with her. But the toddler, apparently frightened by all the noise, was whimpering against his mother's shoulder. Or perhaps he was hungry. Meg remembered Alan, as a boy, making such noises whenever mealtime drew near.

She pulled the apple out of her pocket. Was the child old enough to eat it? Might she offend the mother by offering it? Meg stood and made her way back through the carriage as it jostled her to and fro. When she reached the twosome, she held out her gift, such as it was—free of bruises anyway and a good size for a red pippin.

"Oh!" The mother's eyes widened. "Look what the kind lady has brought you." When she took the apple with a nod of thanks, the toddler wiped his nose with his sleeve, his misery forgotten. She beamed at him. "Mum will take a bite, then share it with you, aye?"

Meg watched them, touched by the way the mother carefully bit into the fruit, peeled away the skin, then fed her son. He was none too patient with the process until his mother made a game of hiding each bite and then producing it with a look of astonishment.

"You were brave to stay aboard the train with your son," Meg said, surveying all the empty seats.

The woman kissed her son's head, then looked up. "My husband works in Edinburgh and cannot come home for Christmas. So we thought we'd surprise him. We'll be there in less than an hour, aye?" She smiled at her boy chewing on another bit of apple. "Thanks to you, miss, our son won't arrive hungry."

"I'm so glad." With a lighter heart Meg returned to her seat, reminding herself it was a simple gesture. Nothing to be proud of. But she *was,* a little.

Meanwhile, the other passenger was buried in his newspaper again, though he never moved his head or turned the page. Meg sympathized with the gentleman. Hadn't she also tried reading, to no avail? He looked to be a few years older than she was. Slender yet muscular, he was no doubt a sportsman. And a bit untidy. His bag was unbuckled, with papers sticking out at all angles. Newspapers, mostly.

Beyond the safe confines of their carriage, the snow was hidden by the darkness except when a lantern posted on the line briefly illuminated a portion of the stark, white landscape. Fir trees bowed low beneath the weight, the branches leaning perilously close to the tracks.

Their progress was slow and halting, as if the engine were dragging the carriages over a bed of rocks rather than along smooth steel rails. Each time the train abruptly paused, then lurched forward, Meg gripped the wooden armrest lest she careen into the aisle. After a few minutes the gentleman across from her put away his *Stirling Observer* and pressed his traveling bag hard against his side.

Larbert station was six miles down the line, with at least one deep cutting in the terrain between here and there. Meg eyed the ice-shrouded window next to her. None of the familiar landmarks would be visible en route. Even the tunnels would be more felt than seen.

As the minutes ticked by, the train seemed to pick up speed. Nothing close to its usual pace but somewhat faster. Meg reached for her satchel, hoping her lesson plans for next term might distract her. When the gentleman glanced in her direction with an inquiring look on his face, she offered a slight nod in return. *I am well, sir. Kind of you to be concerned.*

Meg looked at her watch again. She'd be home no later than seven, maybe half past—

Her bag suddenly toppled into the aisle as she was thrown against the seat in front of her, shoulder first. The train shuddered. A terrible sound, like iron meeting ice, reverberated through the carriage, then silence. Stunned, Meg slumped forward, aware only of a searing pain and a little boy crying for his mother.

Chapter Four

A hero is a man who
does what he can.

ROMAIN ROLLAND

Gordon shook his head, dazed for a moment. How had he ended up on his knees, halfway into the aisle?

Then he remembered the train coming to a violent stop and his fleeting awareness of their having hit something. He took his time standing, wanting to be sure he'd fully recovered his balance, then looked about the dimly lit carriage to see if the other passengers had fallen as well.

Indeed they had. Judging by the way Miss Campbell was gingerly holding her shoulder, she'd been bruised. Or worse. "Are you quite all right, miss?"

She nodded slightly. "Might you see to the child?"

He eased his way down the aisle to where the boy lay on his back, limbs flailing. Gordon rescued him at once and deposited the wriggling lad onto the seat beside his mother. "How else might I help, madam?"

She winced as she tried to sit up, one leg pinned beneath the seat at an awkward angle. "I'm afraid—"

"Yes, I see," Gordon said evenly, not wanting to alarm her.

Miss Campbell was now on her feet and moving toward them. "If you will, sir, please locate the conductor while I tend to Mrs...."

"Mrs. Reid," the woman offered, her voice thin. "And my boy, Tam."

Gordon made a hasty exit before either of them inquired after his name. It seemed Miss Campbell had yet to recognize him. How old had she been? Thirteen? Fourteen? If she learned his surname, would it likely stir her memory?

No point worrying about such things now. Whatever had happened to the train, the news would not be good.

Gordon opened the carriage door, then cautiously stepped down onto the railway bed. The night wind flapped his coat about his legs like a flag on a pole. Snow as sharp as icicles stabbed every area of exposed skin—the back of his neck, the narrow gap between sleeve and glove, the upper half of his face. He fought his way forward, chin pressed against his chest, as he grasped the outer handrails for support, keenly aware of the steep drop-off less than a foot to his right.

When he reached one of the small first-class compartments, Gordon climbed up to the door with some difficulty, then yanked it open, sending snow cascading down from the roof and onto his shoulders.

"Come, man!" A well-dressed gentleman motioned him inside, clearly unconcerned with Gordon's disheveled appearance. "Have you a report for us?"

"We've need of a doctor in second class," Gordon said without preamble. "Two women, one slightly injured, the other more so, I fear." He looked at the anxious faces of the three passengers. "Do you know what's happened?"

"We rather hoped you might tell us," an elderly gentleman confided. "In the meantime, Dr. Johnstone here could see to the ladies."

A bright-eyed fellow, no older than twenty-five, was already buttoning his coat and reaching for the brown medical bag at his feet. The leather sides were unscratched, and the brass buckles gleamed in the lamplight.

"A Mrs. Reid and a Miss Campbell," Gordon told him. "You'll want to see what's needed in third class as well."

Johnstone left at once, his eagerness to be of service palpable.

"I'm headed for the engine," Gordon told the rest of them.

Seconds later he was covered in fresh snow as he stumbled past another first-class compartment and then the tender heaped with coal. When he reached the cab, neither the engineer nor the fireman was at his station. Moving to the front of the train, he found the men and discovered the problem as well: the front half of the engine was buried in a massive snowdrift.

A faint shaft of light from the fireman's lantern made the grim situation clear. The locomotive had entered a deep cutting where the high sides served to trap the snowfall. Strong northerly winds had done the rest, creating a shoulder-high wall of snow that was invisible in the storm.

Gordon shouted into the wind, "Can it be cleared, sir?"

"Too soon to tell." The engineer grunted as he heaved aside another shovelful. "I've faced drifts like this before. But not in many years. And not on Christmas Eve, when we're short-handed."

Gordon looked about for the conductor. "Where's McGregor?"

"Third class," the fireman answered, "looking for laborers to dig us out. A signalman has already left on foot, taking word back to Stirling." He eyed Gordon over his wire-rimmed glasses. "Will you help us, sir?"

Gordon knew his dress boots weren't fit for the task, his calfskin gloves were too thin, and the woolen scarf he'd mistakenly left on the morning train would be sorely missed.

He reached for a shovel poking out of the drift. "Show me where to start."

The combination of wet, heavy snow and bitterly cold winds made for rough going. When help arrived from the other carriages, there weren't enough shovels, so men dug with metal trays, with coal buckets, with anything they could find to move the snow. The lanterns scattered about were of little use other than to show the men how much had yet to be accomplished.

Gordon lost all sense of time as he thrust his shovel into the snow again and again, his back protesting, the muscles in his arms and shoulders straining with every load. If they could clear enough snow, they might yet reach Edinburgh that night. Miss Campbell and he could go their separate ways. The past would remain undisturbed and his shame with it.

But his conscience refused to be silenced. *You wanted to apologize twelve years ago. Why not do so tonight?*

The very idea made his face grow hot, causing him to feel the sting of the wind even more acutely. What would he say to the woman after all this time? How would he begin? *My name is Gordon Shaw. A dozen years ago I did an unforgivable thing…*

But wasn't that what he wanted? Forgiveness?

Gordon heaved a fresh pile of snow into the air, wishing he might dispense with the weight of his guilt half so easily. No words, however sincere, could undo what had happened that night. Confessing his sins now would only open old wounds. Had he not done enough damage?

Fueled by frustration, he jammed his shovel into the snowdrift. What was the point of asking someone's forgiveness if it changed nothing?

Gordon labored in stony silence, unwilling to acknowledge the storm that raged within him. Once the engine was freed from its snowy prison, he would be southbound—incentive enough to keep shoveling.

After two long hours McGregor met briefly with his engineer, then called a halt to their efforts. "You've done your best, men," the conductor informed his weary volunteers. "Alas, I've just learned the piston rod did not withstand the impact. We cannot move forward or backward."

All their shoveling had been for naught.

Gordon steeled himself. He knew what was coming next.

"Carry what bags you can, and leave the others," the conductor told them. "One of my men is staying behind to guard the train. The rest of us will head for Stirling on foot."

Gordon started toward second class, tamping down his fears. He could walk back with some of the men and avoid Miss Campbell altogether. Once he reached Stirling, lodging might be found at the Coffee House at the head of Baker Street. He would manage there for the night, then slip out of town the moment the railway was back in service—

No. Gordon slowed his steps. *That's not how it's going to be, Shaw. Not this time.*

He kept walking, though the voice continued to prod him.

You've carried this burden long enough. What are you waiting for?

He was waiting for the right time. And that time was not tonight.

Gordon pulled himself up to the carriage entrance with a grunt, then flung open the door harder than he meant to. It banged against the exterior of the carriage, scaring little Tam, who began to wail.

Gordon quickly closed the door behind him, sorry he'd been so thoughtless. "I didn't mean to frighten the boy."

"Of course you didn't." Miss Campbell looked up with a faint smile on her face, then smoothed her hand across Tam's downy head, settling him at once. "You must be exhausted from shoveling snow."

He shrugged, not wanting to admit it.

It seemed she had things well in hand. Their various traveling bags were tucked back under their seats, and Mrs. Reid was wrapped in one of the blankets from the storage compartment, her heels propped on a foot warmer filled with fresh coals. "Compliments of Dr. Johnstone," Miss Campbell explained. "Are we leaving, then?"

"Aye, but not aboard the train." Gordon hesitated, gauging her reaction. "We'll be walking back to Stirling."

"Oh dear." Her blue eyes shone with concern. "Mrs. Reid's injury will not allow it. And her son cannot walk such a distance."

"Then I'll carry him," Gordon said without a moment's thought. He couldn't remember the last time he'd looked after a child. Surely it wouldn't be too difficult. "As for you, Mrs. Reid, a large blanket will suffice for a hammock. I daresay the men will vie for the honor of bearing you home."

"I'm not so light a burden as my son," the woman protested.

He noted her petite frame. "Light enough, madam."

Within minutes Gordon had joined the twenty-odd passengers convened on the tracks and had found two able men to carry Mrs. Reid. She tolerated their less-than-gentle handling and seemed comfortable enough cocooned inside her blanket. With his traveling bag and Miss Campbell's satchel in one hand and a sleepy lad wrapped in his own small blanket and draped over his shoulder, Gordon waited impatiently for the conductor's signal to start back.

At least the northerly wind had lost its cruel bite. The dense snow was merely falling rather than blowing in their faces. Though they had perhaps three miles to cover, if they followed the rails, they'd not get lost.

Miss Campbell seemed fretful about leaving her trunk until McGregor assured her it would be delivered to her door once the train returned to Stirling station. "Your family lives on Albert Place, aye?"

"They do, but"—she bit her lip—"it might be best to store my trunk at the station. I plan to take the first train bound for Edinburgh."

"Hard to say when that might be, miss."

The conductor turned to address other needs, leaving Gordon to ponder what he'd just heard. Twelve years ago the Campbells had resided on Spittal Street in a far less prestigious home than the fine sandstone houses of Albert Place, just beyond the town wall. Surely they had room for their daughter. Did she not wish to spend Christmas with her family?

What are you running from, Miss Campbell? Gordon knew he had no business posing such a question. Not when he was on the run himself.

Then stop running, Shaw. Gordon looked down at the toes of his boots. Could he do so? Stop fleeing from his past and simply face it? Confess who he was and what he'd done?

Be strong and of a good courage. A gentler voice this time, stirring deep inside him. *Be not afraid, neither be thou dismayed.*

Gordon could ignore his conscience, but he could not disregard the Almighty. He lifted his head, holding little Tam close. *You'll help me, Lord? Show me what to do, tell me what to say?* Gordon was not afraid of words; they were his livelihood. But an apology for so great an error would not be easily spoken.

The LORD thy God is with thee whithersoever thou goest. Aye, there was comfort in that. Especially with a long walk ahead of him and a meeting with the Campbells to follow. If they allowed him across their threshold, that is.

At last the travelers began heading north. On a warm, moonlit evening, it would have been a pleasant walk. Not so on this dark night. Their steps labored, their voices subdued, the group slowly moved forward, no more than two abreast between the silvery rails, which were barely visible beneath the shifting snow. A dozen portable lanterns were scattered up and down the line, though the light they offered was meager at best.

Gordon concentrated on remaining upright, ever mindful of the child entrusted to his care. The boy was lighter than expected and warm. With Tam's arm circling his neck, Gordon no longer missed his scarf. The child's mother was directly behind them, snug in her makeshift hammock.

Miss Campbell fell into step beside him—wanting to be near the boy, he imagined. Or close to her satchel. She was shorter in stature than he'd first thought. The brim of her hat barely reached his shoulder. "Pardon me for not offering my arm, Miss Campbell."

She lifted her head and gave him a tentative smile. "I believe we can overlook such courtesies tonight."

No sooner were the words spoken than she lost her footing. With a startled cry, she grabbed his coat sleeve, nearly pulling him down with her, the sharp incline on either side of the tracks dangerously near.

Hugging the boy tightly to his chest, Gordon dropped both bags and reached for her other hand. "I have you, miss!" He jammed his boot against the inside of the steel rail, determined to keep all three of them from tumbling down the icy embankment.

She clung to his arm until she regained her balance, then slowly let go of him, gratitude in her eyes. "Now I must beg *your* pardon, sir."

"Not at all," Gordon said, holding her gaze.

It is your forgiveness I must seek, Miss Campbell. And your family's. Tonight.

Chapter Five

No one knows the weight
of another's burden.

GEORGE HERBERT

M eg's cheeks grew warm beneath her scarf. How boldly this gentleman looked at her! As if he knew her, though their paths had not crossed before this afternoon. He'd overheard Mr. McGregor address her, then took the liberty of using her name without offering his own. An oversight? Or was it intentional?

She should be offended. Refuse to speak with him.

But he'd been so helpful to Mrs. Reid and to the railway and had just spared her from a nasty fall. Who could think ill of such a gentleman? In time he would realize he'd neglected to share his name. Why embarrass him further by pointing out his mistake? She was certainly grateful to have him within arm's reach, for the going was hazardous, and Stirling was a long way off.

Holding her arms out a bit to keep her balance, Meg studied him as they tramped through the snow together. His gray wool suit gave no solid clue regarding his profession, though his neatly trimmed beard and polished boots marked him as a gentleman. And a handsome one, with his fine, long nose and strong chin.

He was not a civil servant, she decided, or a clerk who handled money, like her father, who had been employed by the Royal Bank since before she was born. Rather, this man depended upon his intellect for his income. She was certain of it. Something about his eyes, his high forehead. Was he a solicitor, perhaps? Handling wills, estates, conveyances, and the like?

Meg's curiosity got the better of her. The gentleman might be a stranger, but in such circumstances one was permitted to speak a bit more freely.

"Tell me, sir, are you from Stirling or Edinburgh?" she asked, thinking one end of the line or the other would likely be his home.

He didn't answer immediately. "Glasgow," he finally said.

Not the answer she'd expected, yet the industrial town suited him. Lean. Energetic. Maybe if she revealed something of her life, he would follow her lead. "Stirling is my childhood home," she told him, "but I've lived in Edinburgh for the last six years."

A good bit of information. *Your turn, sir.*

When he didn't respond to her volley as swiftly as she wished, Meg pressed on, throwing propriety aside as if it were a soiled pair of gloves. "Might you have business in Edinburgh? Or do you have family there, awaiting your arrival for Christmas?"

"I have…" He slowed his steps to look at her. "I have no family in Edinburgh, but I do have business there, aye."

When other passengers began closing in from behind, he lengthened his stride, and she did the same. Their shoulders were a hand's-breadth apart—a necessity if they meant to stay between the rails. It also allowed them to converse without being overheard by the entire group. She sensed the gentleman wanted that.

"Business, you say?" she prompted him.

After a long pause he said, "I write for the *Glasgow Herald.*"

Meg hid her surprise. A newspaperman? She would not have guessed that. A respectable occupation, at least in most circles. Certainly the *Herald* was above reproach.

"That's why I was in Stirling today," he explained, "interviewing the new editor of the *British Messenger.*"

Meg nodded with approval. The Drummonds, one of Stirling's most respected families, published the monthly magazine.

She pictured the three-story building on Dumbarton Road with its impressive bank of windows. "You were quite near my parents' house."

"On Albert Place," he affirmed, then began stumbling over his words. "You said... That is, I believe Mr. McGregor mentioned your address."

Aye, and my name too. He missed very little, this tall newspaperman from Glasgow.

Meg looked about, taking in what she could of their surroundings. How quiet and still their frozen world had become! The snow fell in utter silence, and the air sounded hollow, as if they were standing in the midst of a great cathedral, its vaulted ceiling stretching toward heaven.

"Christmas Eve," she said on a sigh, her warm breath visible. "I shall miss all the candles in Edinburgh's windows."

"At least we have light." He nodded toward the bobbing lanterns carried by laborers and gentry alike. "Once we reach Stirling, I imagine you'll see plenty of candles burning around King's Park."

Meg heard a coolness in his tone at the mention of her neighborhood. Did he think less of her family for living in the fashionable part of Stirling? She didn't entirely approve of it herself, and not just because the move was Alan's idea. Her father was a middling bank clerk—a stable position but not a highly lucrative one. Purchasing even the smallest house in

King's Park had taken all his earnings and every penny of her mother's inheritance.

I could have helped them if I'd sold Aunt Jean's house.

She pushed aside the nagging thought. "Our cottage has only two windows facing the street," she told him, "but the villas on Victoria Square will have a glittering array of candles."

Though he merely nodded, she saw something flicker in his brown eyes, as if he'd formed one opinion and now was discarding it for another.

"I imagine your family will be surprised to see you," he said.

Her throat tightened. *Surprised* wasn't the word that came to mind. Alan would gloat over her being forced to return. Her parents would be relieved yet upset with her for leaving. "They certainly are not expecting me," she admitted.

He said nothing for a moment, as if he were listening to his boots crunch the snow. "Will your family be home this evening?"

An odd question, Meg thought. Was he concerned about her returning to an empty house?

"Aye, they'll be there," she said, imagining the Campbells at their oblong dining table—her father at the head, her mother at the foot, and Alan seated on his usual side of the table with an extra cushion on his chair, meant to make him more comfortable. Even with the gas chandelier overhead, beeswax candles would be flickering on the mantelpiece.

"Our family dines at eight. My mother prides herself on serving a fine meal on Christmas Eve," Meg told him as vivid recollections of past holidays swept over her. "Roasted pork with apples. Carrots, potatoes, and turnips. Fresh bread tied in a thick braid and drenched in butter…" Her voice trailed off into a melancholy silence. Her place at the table would be empty tonight.

The gentleman beside her said, "No wonder you return home each Christmas."

"But I *don't*." The words poured out before she could stop them. "At least, I haven't, not in years." Was she proud of that fact? Or ashamed? "My home is in Edinburgh now. My work is there. My dearest friends are there. But my family…" She fought to regain her composure. "My family is…"

"I understand, Miss Campbell. More than you know." His shoulder lightly brushed against hers as they quietly walked in tandem. "Tell me why you've stopped coming home."

Could she do so? The temptation overwhelmed her. To speak honestly without the fear of hurting anyone. To open her heart to a stranger who knew nothing of her family and would leave town in the morning, carrying her secrets with him.

Meg drew a long, steadying breath and looked straight ahead, convinced if she gazed into those warm, chestnut-colored eyes, she would feel exposed and stop at once. Whatever she found the courage to tell him, it would be easier if she saw nothing but the steady snowfall and the backs of two passengers, now several yards ahead.

She shivered, suddenly more aware of the cold, and tugged her hat firmly on her head. "I have a brother named Alan." That seemed the place to begin. He was at the heart of the issue, wasn't he? "I was four when he was born." Even as she sought the right words, she wondered if this gentleman could possibly grasp how a single event had the power to alter a family forever.

For most of her young life, Meg had been her father's favorite, though she'd tried not to notice. But Alan had. As he grew, so did his resentment. Then everything changed on that January afternoon.

In the end Meg simply said, "When my brother was ten years of age, he was badly injured."

The gentleman frowned. "What happened?"

"An accident. My parents weren't there, but I was."

As Meg described the scene at the curling pond, her walking companion leaned closer, his expression strangely intent. "An inebriated young man began swinging his curling stone," she explained. "When it slipped from his grasp, the stone struck my brother in the back." She could still recall the awful thud as the stone fell to the ice.

After a moment he asked, "Did you learn the man's name?"

"Gordon Shaw," she said without hesitation. "I was only fourteen, so I recall little else about him. But I could hardly forget the name of someone who ruined my brother's life."

His response was slow in coming. "I am…sorry, Miss Campbell."

Meg shook her head, knowing the truth. "It was my fault too." How she hated putting that into words! "I was the older sister, meant to watch Alan. If I'd paid closer attention… If I'd kept him off the ice…"

She pressed her lips together, trying to stem the painful memories. Alan's head resting on her lap, tears streaming down his cheeks. Her father's grief. *How could you let this happen?* Her mother's sorrow. *My boy, my poor boy.* Meg had cried herself to sleep that night and many nights thereafter. Blaming a stranger for being careless. Blaming herself as well.

"Your brother's injury," the gentleman prompted her. "Was it serious?"

"At first Alan couldn't stand. Couldn't move, really. A neighbor took us home in his sleigh. Dr. Bayne was summoned at once and deemed my brother stricken with paralysis."

For a stranger, his dismay was marked. "Your brother is bedridden, then."

"Not entirely. With assistance he can stand, but he cannot walk on his own."

Meg was reluctant to say more on the subject for fear of

sounding uncharitable. Still, over the years it seemed Alan had made the most of his affliction, seeking sympathy from every quarter. Mum waited on him hand and foot. Father showered him with presents and required nothing of him. Her brother did no work of any kind but simply sat in his favorite chair and ordered their parents about—

Forgive me, Alan. Her assessment, however accurate, was unkind. Even though he had been more difficult than usual today, he deserved her compassion.

"Of course I feel sorry for my brother," she said, "and guilty as well. Of the two of us, I am the healthy one."

The gentleman beside her nodded as if he grasped what she was saying. "When you're not the one injured, that can be a burden too."

"Aye, it can." Meg was so relieved to find someone who understood that she spilled out the rest. "Sadly, Alan has grown more disagreeable with each passing season. The year I turned twenty, I moved to Edinburgh to care for my aunt Jean. In all honesty, I could not escape my brother's company quickly enough."

There. She had put the awful truth into words.

When the gentleman did not respond, Meg's heart sank. He surely thought less of her now that she'd spoken so frankly. If he had no siblings of his own, he'd not likely comprehend how it was with Alan and her. A certain measure of love, aye, but not always loyalty or affection. At least not since his accident.

She braved the question. "Do you have brothers or sisters?"

"I have no family at all." His words were void of emotion. "My parents moved south to England and died of pneumonia one cold, wet spring."

Meg turned to him, aghast. "Here I am, filling your ears with my troubles when you've suffered far more."

"You have no need to apologize, Miss Campbell. Not to me."

Looking into his eyes, she saw a well of sadness that touched her deeply. "We've made a grave error, you and I." She lightly rested her hand on his forearm. "It's time we were properly introduced. I am Miss Margaret Campbell. Might I be so bold as to ask your name, sir?"

"My name?" His gaze no longer met hers.

Chapter Six

I watched her face to see which way
She took the awful news.

EMILY DICKINSON

Gordon lifted his head, forcing himself to look at her. "I am Mr. Gordon…" His surname stuck in his throat. *Say it, man. She deserves to know.* "Mr. Gordon…"

"Gordon?" A smile lit her countenance. "Is that so? I knew a Gordon family once. They lived near our old house on Spittal Street." She tipped her head, eying him more closely. "Black haired, all of them. Not relatives of yours, I imagine."

"No…no, I'm…" He hesitated one second too long.

Margaret Campbell was facing forward now. "Pardon me,

Mr. Gordon. I should have inquired about your surname long before this. Rather an awkward situation, I'm afraid."

Awkward? Gordon's limbs felt so weak he feared Tam might slip from his grasp. *Mr. Gordon.* How had such a thing happened? *Foolish question, Shaw.* He'd let it happen. Let her think he was someone else. A stranger worth knowing instead of someone her family despised.

Do something. Say something. "Forgive me, but—"

A woman's voice called out, "Miss Campbell, if I may?"

When she turned to respond, Gordon had no choice but to do the same.

The men carrying Mrs. Reid lumbered up. Both were red faced and breathing hard with their patient sagging between them.

She peered at them from her wool hammock. "I fear my kind stretcher-bearers are in need of a respite." When the men protested, she offered a faint smile but would not be dissuaded. Instead, she looked fondly at her son, then at Gordon. "Sir, might you find two other men willing to take a turn? It is a great deal to ask—"

"Not at all, madam." He took off at once, needing time to think, to find a way to undo what he'd done. More to the point, what he'd *not* done.

The best solution was the simplest one. The instant he was alone with Margaret Campbell, he would tell her the truth: *My name is Gordon Shaw.* He said those words every day of his life. Surely he could say them now when it truly mattered.

She'd shared her name, hadn't she? *Margaret.* Though he was not free to use her Christian name, he preferred to think of her that way. *Margaret.* A traditional name. It suited her.

Your name suits you as well, Shaw. Say it.

His face hot, Gordon stamped up the line thirty yards until he located two fresh recruits willing to help. He led them back toward Mrs. Reid, trying not to jostle the child up and down as he went. But by the time they reached her, the boy was fully awake and crying for his mother.

Well done, Shaw. It seemed he couldn't even look after a small child without making a hash of things. Gordon gently lowered the boy so his mother might comfort him face to face.

"I cannot hold you just now, dear lad," she told him, cupping his pudgy cheeks with her hands. "But you are being well taken care of by Mr....ah..."

When he didn't answer quickly enough, Margaret said, "His name is Gordon."

The Reid woman beamed up at him. "Thank you again, Mr. Gordon."

He smiled through clenched teeth. *Shaw. My name is Shaw.* He could hardly state so now with a dozen people standing about. Margaret might be embarrassed, thinking the mistake was hers, and the others would surely be confused. Once the group dispersed and everyone was out of earshot, he would put things right.

But Gordon hadn't counted on little Tam Reid.

Duly rested after his nap, the child bounced up and down in Gordon's arms, then tried to capture snowflakes between his tiny mittens, all the while babbling away.

"What a darling boy." Margaret smiled at him as they walked, clearly enchanted.

Gordon, meanwhile, was trying to keep his tweed cap out of the child's reach lest he send it flying into the night. Minutes later when Tam nearly leaped into a snowdrift, Gordon decided the child needed to stretch his legs. He lowered him to the ground, then used a bag in each hand to corral the lad as they walked between the rails.

The attempt was not entirely successful.

After the boy stumbled several times and landed face-first in the snow, Margaret finally said, "Mr. Gordon, this will never do," and swept Tam into her embrace. She brushed away his tears and soon had him giggling again. "My students are a few years older, but I believe I can manage one toddler. Isn't that so, Tam?"

Gordon groaned inwardly. However charming the lad, his presence made a serious conversation difficult, if not impossible. But that was no excuse. The truth could not wait a moment longer.

He matched her stride, walking as close as he dared. "Miss Campbell, I have not been entirely honest with you."

"Oh?" She looked up at him expectantly. Then a distant church bell began to toll, and she counted the hours under her breath. "Is it only nine o'clock? I thought surely it must be midnight."

Gordon cared little about the hour. What mattered was they were halfway to Stirling, and he was running out of time. *Make haste to help me.* A short prayer and a desperate one.

He gripped their bags, strengthening his resolve. "I too have stayed away from Stirling. Far longer than you, Miss Campbell, and for good reason."

Her eyes widened. "Is Stirling your home as well?"

"It was, until I was seventeen." He cleared his throat. "Then I...hurt someone without meaning to. A young boy of ten."

The slightest intake of air. "Just like my brother."

"Exactly like him, Miss Campbell."

There was no going back now. Gordon slowed to a stop, then turned to her, wanting to see her expression when the truth sank in and the punishment he so richly deserved would be meted out. "It was your brother, Alan, whom I injured. On a curling pond in King's Park twelve years ago."

She wrinkled her brow. "But your name is..."

"Mr. Gordon Shaw."

The pain etched on her face was worse than he'd imagined.

Almost more than he could bear. Her chin trembled, and her blue eyes glistened with tears as she tried to speak but could not.

"Aye, Miss Campbell. As you rightly said, I am the man who ruined your brother's life."

"And mine," she whispered.

Chapter Seven

Disappointment tracks
the steps of hope.

LETITIA ELIZABETH LANDON

W hy did you not tell me before? *Why?*" Meg turned away. She didn't want an answer. Not from Gordon Shaw.

"Miss Campbell, if I may ask—"

"You may not." Meg buried her face in Tam's soft woolen bonnet. To think she'd unburdened her heart to this man! Taken him into her confidence. Shared how her brother's injury had affected the family, affected her. *This* man, of all men, had let her talk on and on yet kept his identity a secret.

She lifted her head and promptly strode off, her steps more

resolute than graceful. She dare not stumble, not with Tam in her arms. But she would not stay and hear Gordon Shaw justify his duplicity.

Why had she not put the pieces together and realized who he was before he confessed it? *Because I didn't wish to. Because I was enjoying his company.* She stopped in her tracks as the truth heated her cheeks afresh.

A moment later Mr. Shaw was beside her. "I am grateful you waited—"

"I did nothing of the kind." Meg shifted Tam in her arms. The line of passengers now stretched some distance up and down the rails. Just as well, or they might get an earful if Mr. Shaw did not leave her alone.

Had she looked more closely and listened more carefully, she might have recognized him. True, he'd not had a beard all those years ago. But his hair was the same bright shade, not easily forgotten. She should have known him. She should have *known.*

"Miss Campbell, I do not expect—"

"Then you'll not be disappointed."

Meg hated the harshness in her tone, but she couldn't help it. *Gordon Shaw.* How dare he endear himself to her! For years her family had spoken this man's name with contempt. Did he think their heartache could be swept away with a simple apology? She was glad for the darkness, for the cold, for the snow.

Even with Mr. Shaw walking right beside her, she could pretend he wasn't there.

Unfortunately, he kept talking. "I am entirely to blame for your brother's condition, Miss Campbell. Discard any notion that you were responsible."

She glared up at him. "In the same manner you discarded your curling stone? Tossing it across the ice without considering where it might land?"

He looked as if he'd just been slapped. "Miss Campbell, I know—"

"And *I* know that my brother was innocent and that you were not. *Are* not," she amended. "I suppose you recognized me aboard the train?"

"Aye." He didn't flinch or look away. "Even before we left Stirling station, I realized you were Alan's sister."

"And yet you said nothing?"

"To my great shame, I did not. Not even when you mistook my surname for Gordon." Though weighed down by their bags, he spread his hands in a gesture of surrender. "Whether from fear or cowardice, I have done you a great disservice, Miss Campbell. Can you possibly forgive me?"

"*Forgive* you?" The sincerity of his expression merely heightened her pique. "I cannot think of one reason—" Meg bit back the rest, ashamed of her vitriol. She could at least be civil even if she chose not to forgive him.

Is forgiveness a matter of choice? She frowned, irritated by the question. "At the moment my only concern is reaching home."

When she stamped off, Meg felt a rush of cold air on her neck and realized little Tam had loosened her scarf. "Come, lad, what are you up to?" she scolded him lightly, tucking the woolen fabric back in place. She glanced at Mrs. Reid, well behind them now, then hugged the child to her heart, patently ignoring Gordon Shaw. "We shall have you and your mum safe and warm within the hour."

The snowfall at last had eased. Not far ahead the lights of Stirling twinkled like stars, from the castle to the mill lade. However fine the view, her hands were numb, her walking boots were soaked through, and she could not feel her toes.

Gordon's voice was low but steadier than she expected. "Miss Campbell, may I ask what you intend to do when we reach Stirling?"

She spoke plainly. "Knock on my parents' door and hope they will have room in their hearts for a foolish daughter."

"Perhaps I might escort you home—"

"Certainly not!" Meg stared at him, aghast.

"But I would very much like to meet them," he explained. "To apologize—"

"No!" Meg covered Tam's ear and pressed him against her lest the urgency in her voice frighten him. "It is too late, Mr. Shaw. You cannot make amends now."

"Nonetheless, I mean to try."

"Please, it is out of the question," Meg told him. "I cannot think what my brother would say if you appeared on our doorstep." *Nor what Alan might say to me.* "It simply will not do for you to come to our house, Mr. Shaw, and dredge up painful memories best forgotten. Christmas is meant to be joyful, is it not?"

When he dropped back a step, Meg felt the tension inside her begin to ease. Perhaps he finally understood.

She pressed on, focusing her thoughts on a warm fire, a plate of food, and a clean bed. Even so, Gordon's wounded expression was firmly planted in her mind.

At last the lights of Stirling station came into view. Exuberant cries rang up and down the line. "Almost there, almost home," Meg whispered in Tam's ear. She heard the stragglers behind them making an effort to catch up as she found her own steps growing lighter, swifter.

Then she saw the lanterns and the faces and the open arms. "Look, Tam!" she cried, turning the child so he could see. "Look at all the people coming down the track to greet us."

The boy squealed, clapping and waving, as a spirited band of people drew near, lanterns held high, the light reflecting off the snow. Wives welcomed husbands with warm blankets and heartfelt embraces while the railway staff pointed the way to hot tea in the booking office.

The stationmaster, resplendent in his dark uniform with its gleaming brass buttons, guided Meg up the narrow steps onto the crowded platform, brightly lit and swept clear of snow. "Many apologies, madam," he said, eying Tam. "You and your boy have had a rough night of it."

"Oh, this fine lad belongs to Mrs. Reid." Meg stepped aside to make room for the two men cautiously lifting the injured mother onto the platform with Dr. Johnstone in close attendance.

An older woman rushed forward with a cry of alarm. "Emma, my dear girl! Whatever has happened to you?" With the same coloring, the same expressive features, she was certainly Mrs. Reid's mother.

Dr. Johnstone, for propriety's sake, whispered his diagnosis in the older woman's ear. She listened with furrowed brow, then nodded, looking relieved. "And here's my wee Tam, come to spend Christmas with his granny after all." She collected the lad without ceremony, thanking Meg as she did, then directed the small party toward a waiting carriage beyond the station doors.

Meg watched the child disappear from sight, feeling bereft. Would she ever see Tam again? Emma Reid had intended to surprise her husband in Edinburgh. Instead she'd returned to Stirling with a badly twisted leg and a tired little boy. "Mr. Reid will come home to us on Hogmanay," she'd told Meg. "We shall celebrate soon enough."

For a brief moment Meg imagined what it would be like to have someone who dearly loved her waiting at the end of a railway line. Over the years she'd grown accustomed to arriving at the Princes Street station with no one to greet her, then unlocking the door to her empty house and making tea for one. But it would be lovely to be welcomed home.

When she turned to see how the other passengers were faring, Meg found Gordon Shaw standing mere steps behind her. His clothes were rumpled, his hair unkempt, but in his brown eyes a spark of hope still shone.

If he were Mr. Gordon, the gentleman she'd first met, she might extend her hand, warmly wish him a happy Christmas, and anticipate hearing from him in the new year. Perhaps receiving a letter from him in the post. Making plans to have tea together the next time he was in Edinburgh.

But he was Gordon Shaw, the man who'd earned her trust under false pretenses. She would not be seeing him again. Not this year. Not any year.

Chapter Eight

What's past is prologue.

WILLIAM SHAKESPEARE

M eg wanted to turn around, to walk away, but found she could not. Not without saying good-bye.

Gordon removed his tweed cap and brushed away the snow, then slowly tugged it back in place, holding her gaze. "Miss Campbell, I will keep saying I'm sorry until you believe me."

"I do believe you, Mr. Shaw. I'm just not certain I can forgive you."

He dipped his chin in acknowledgment. "Your honesty is refreshing."

And yours is disarming.

Meg saw no point in chastening him further. They would follow separate paths now—she to her parents' house by carriage, if one might be arranged, and he to wherever newspapermen sought lodging.

"Good-bye," she said quietly, then turned before he could offer a parting word in return. It was better that way.

Damp skirt in hand, Meg aimed for the booking office, drawn by the promised cup of tea. She was chilled to the bone and needed something to fortify her, knowing this night was far from over. She still had to face her brother. And apologize to her parents.

Tea first, then a carriage, and the moment she arrived home, a fresh change of clothing. Her garments, unfortunately, were in a trunk on a snowbound train three miles south. Was there something at home she might wear, a gown she'd left behind? It would be many seasons old but blessedly dry.

From across the bustling platform, a familiar voice called out her name.

Meg lifted her brows. *Mum?*

She turned in time to see her mother and father wending their way through the crowd. Had they truly come to meet her even though she'd departed in haste without a kind word to either of them? She lifted her hand, hoping they wouldn't see the tears in her eyes.

Lorna Campbell, her fair-haired mother, was looking especially cheery in her red wool coat. If she harbored any hurt feelings, they were well hidden. Her eyes were bright with excitement and her smile genuine as she hurried up to Meg, hands outstretched.

"Margaret!" Her mother had to stand on tiptoe to kiss her cheeks. "How relieved we are to see you! Aren't we, Mr. Campbell?" When her quiet husband only nodded, she blithely carried on. "You remember Mrs. Corr from Spittal Street? Well! She told us about the frightful accident on the three twenty-six. Frightful. A snowdrift, she said. Taller than the engine, she said. Her husband works for the railway, you know."

"Aye, Mum." Meg squeezed her mother's hands, exceedingly glad to see her. "I know. And I am sorry that I left—"

"Oh, tut-tut. We've no need to talk about that now." Her mother was clearly more interested in the evening's drama. "The instant the signalman appeared at Stirling station, news spread from the Top of the Town to Port Street. You can imagine what a commotion it caused! Twenty or more passengers stranded in the countryside. Since the porter had stopped by earlier for your trunk, we were certain you were one of them." She looked about, then lowered her voice. "As you can see, the station is filled with curious onlookers. But we came for you, dear Margaret. Just for you."

Meg stole a glance at her father, still dressed for the bank in his white wing collar and top hat. *Have you also come for me, Father?* His expression was blank, as if he'd wiped his features clean with a blackboard eraser. It was his public face, his Royal Bank face. He still loved her; she was certain of it. But Alan's many needs left their father little time to show his affection.

Before they could head toward the doors, the stationmaster reappeared, making his rounds on behalf of the Caledonian Railway. "Well, if it isn't Mr. Robert Campbell." The older man's smile was nearly hidden by his drooping mustache. "I see your daughter has been returned to you safe and sound."

"And wet and cold," her father said evenly. "Couldn't this accident have been prevented?"

"For he saith to the snow, Be thou on the earth." The stationmaster splayed his hands. "It would seem the Almighty wanted snow on Christmas Eve."

No one could take umbrage with that statement. Not even Alan.

"Come, ladies," her father said. "Our carriage is waiting and our dinner as well."

Meg glanced at the station clock. "But it's nearly ten. Have you not—"

"No, dear." Her mother slipped her hand into the crook of Meg's arm. "We delayed our meal until you returned. I think you'll find your brother is most anxious to see you."

So he might have his dinner? Meg discarded the callous

thought at once. Perhaps Alan regretted their earlier exchange and wished to mend things between them, though she hated to pin her hopes on so thin a fabric.

"Miss Campbell?" Gordon Shaw spoke, a mere step behind her. "Beg pardon, but I believe you'll want this."

Meg quickly spun around, realizing he still had her satchel.

"Thank you," she murmured as she retrieved her leather bag from Mr. Shaw's hand. Though his clothes were still badly wrinkled, in a few minutes' time he'd combed his hair, straightened his tie, and made himself reasonably presentable.

Oh no. Meg's hands, already cold inside her gloves, turned to ice. *Is that what he expects? That I'll present him to my parents so he might apologize?*

She turned and found them both looking at him, waiting to be introduced. *Of course.* Her parents had never met Gordon Shaw and had known him only by reputation: a reckless youth with a thatch of bright red hair and spindles for legs. The man standing before them was neither intoxicated nor gangling, and he had done their daughter a kind service, for which he deserved their warmest courtesy.

"Mr. Robert Campbell," her father said with a slight bow. "And my wife, Mrs. Campbell. It seems you've already made our daughter's acquaintance."

She implored Gordon with her eyes. *Do not do this. Do not tell them who you are.*

"Indeed we have met, sir, on the train." He returned her father's bow. "My name is—"

"Mr. Gordon from Glasgow," Meg blurted out, desperate to stop him. She would not let this man upset her family with his belated regrets. She would *not*.

For a moment no one spoke.

Her mother, as effusive as her father was taciturn, put an end to the awkward silence. "For whatever assistance you provided our daughter on her difficult journey home, we do thank you, Mr. Gordon."

"My pleasure, madam."

Meg looked at him, fearing his brown eyes would be filled with contempt. Instead she saw resignation. Because of her, he was Mr. Gordon again. The stab of guilt she felt was well deserved.

"Will you be spending the night with your family?" her mother asked him.

"I have no relations in town," Gordon replied, "so I plan to seek lodging at the Coffee House—"

Her mother gasped. "At the head of Baker Street? No, no, Mr. Gordon. It is not at all suitable for a gentleman."

"You'll find a respectable inn on King Street," her father told him. "Suppose we deliver you there."

As Gordon murmured his thanks, Meg quietly exhaled.

They would arrive at the Golden Lion in a quarter hour, perhaps less. Gordon Shaw would climb out of their carriage and walk out of their lives, and her parents would never know that she'd lied to them.

In the same way this man lied to me. The very same.

"My dear sirs," her mother said with an exaggerated sigh, "where is your Christmas spirit? Hospitality is a hallmark of the season, is it not? Mr. Gordon, you are welcome to come home with us."

"No!" Meg's hand flew to her mouth. "That is...no one would choose to spend Christmas Eve with strangers." She looked at him, pleaded with him. *You cannot come, must not come.*

"Let the gentleman speak for himself," her mother chided.

"Your daughter is correct," Gordon said evenly. "An inn would be best."

"Where you'll dine on cold meat and stale bread?" Her mother made a ladylike sound of disapproval. "Mrs. Corr told me that most of the passengers disembarked before the train left the station. I daresay you won't find a vacant room in Stirling." She patted her husband's arm. "Come, Mr. Campbell, we must convince him."

Her father offered a slight shrug. "You'll find my wife is not quick to surrender."

That was precisely what Meg wanted Gordon Shaw to do: give up any notion of coming home with them. But the hope on his face dashed hers to the ground.

Clearly he intended to go through with it. To walk through their door, see Alan's paralyzed body for himself, reveal his true identity, and beg their forgiveness—all on a cold winter's night with nowhere else to go if he was banished from their home.

Her mother was still pressing him, as any hostess would. "We have a cozy guest room, more than enough food, and plenty of coal to keep you warm. Please say you'll return home with us, Mr. Gordon. Our Christmas will be all the brighter for your company."

"If you insist, madam. But I'll not presume upon your generosity beyond tomorrow morning."

He was nervous. Meg saw it in his eyes, heard it in his voice. Might he yet change his mind and keep his proper name—and his apologies—to himself? She would hold that possibility close to her heart and, when they had a moment alone, urge him to reconsider.

Her father nodded toward the station door. "To the carriage, then."

"Come along, Meg." Her mother slipped her arm around Meg's waist. "We've kept your brother waiting long enough."

Alan.

Meg walked toward the doorway with leaden feet. Why had she not thought of this before now? Alan was the one member of their family who had a talent for remembering names. And faces.

Chapter Nine

Shun delays, they breed remorse.

ROBERT SOUTHWELL

Gordon followed the Campbells into the street, his empty stomach tying itself in knots.

The situation was impossible and entirely of his own doing. He'd deliberately placed himself in their path. Then he'd accepted their offer of hospitality, even with Margaret giving him every opportunity to refuse. What she'd not given him was the chance to claim his own name. *Mr. Gordon.* Did she mean to spare him? Or to punish him?

"I do hope you like roasted pork," Mrs. Campbell was

saying as they dodged horse-drawn carriages and wagons, all covered with a heavy blanket of snow.

"I will gladly dine on anything you serve," Gordon replied absently, trying to remember when or what he'd last eaten.

When Mr. Campbell reached their hired carriage—a serviceable model pulled by two Cleveland Bays—he offered a hand to his wife and daughter. Gordon climbed in after them and sat across from Margaret, who would not meet his gaze. He knew she was unhappy with him and no doubt exhausted, as he was. And frozen through.

The bricks at their feet having lost their warmth, the interior felt colder than the outdoors. As the carriage pulled away, Gordon drew his coat tighter around him and leaned toward the window. By morning the town might be reduced to a muddy slush, but at the moment the streets of Stirling were clean and white beneath the fresh snowfall.

"Lovely, isn't it?" Mrs. Campbell said. "The street lamps look like moons hung above the pavement."

"Aye, they do." Gordon straightened, trying to think of what else he might say. He'd never been good at small talk. Like most newspapermen, he asked questions, he listened, and he took notes. The only thing on his mind right now was Alan. He'd never expected to see him again. Would he recognize the young boy from long ago?

Mrs. Campbell interrupted his thoughts. "So, Mr. Gordon, suppose you tell us about the accident."

His head shot up. So did Margaret's. *The accident?*

"We'd like a firsthand account." Mrs. Campbell looked at him expectantly. "Was the snowdrift truly higher than the engine?"

His heart eased its frantic thumping. "Not quite so high as that, madam, but high enough." Gordon described the railway mishap in detail while the carriage slowly traveled along the same streets he'd walked that morning. The shops of Murray Place were long closed now, their awnings lowered, their windows dark.

When they slowed to turn onto Dumbarton Road, he glanced at the Drummond Tract Depot, home of the *British Messenger*. Difficult as it was to imagine, he'd been inside that building not ten hours earlier. If someone had told him then where he'd find himself now, Gordon would have laughed at the absurdity of it.

Instead, he looked grimly ahead as each doorway came into view. Soon they would pass Glebe Avenue. Albert Place was next. The carriage would stop, the Campbells would disembark, and the truth would finally be spoken.

My name is Gordon Shaw. A dozen years ago I did an unforgivable thing...

His head throbbed, and his chest ached. By the time they reached their destination, Gordon feared his knees might not hold him. Whatever happened this night, it could not be worse than the last quarter hour.

"Here we are." Mr. Campbell nodded at the door. "If you would, Mr. Gordon."

He quit the stuffy carriage at once, needing room to breathe, to think. As Mr. Campbell helped his wife and daughter step out, Gordon waited for them, traveling bag in hand, beside the wrought-iron gate. Their sandstone cottage was smaller than he'd imagined, with a low hedgerow enclosing the front garden and a high-pitched roof. He detected a slight movement at one of the ornamented windows. Was it a servant, anxious to serve their dinner? Or Alan, curious to see who'd come home with his family?

"Accompany our guest to the door, dear," Mrs. Campbell said, waving Margaret forward.

Gordon fell into step with her as they walked up the shoveled path side by side, much the same way they'd traveled between the rails. He was careful not to brush against her and kept his thoughts to himself. *I am very sorry, Margaret, but I must go through with this.*

A gaslit globe illuminated the single brass number of the cottage. Just before the door swung open, Margaret whispered discreetly, "We must speak. Soon."

Disoriented by her nearness, Gordon nearly stumbled over the threshold. She had made her wishes clear earlier. What more was there to say?

Mrs. Campbell sang out from behind him, "Mr. Gordon, this is our Clara."

The young maidservant ushered him in, her eyes bright, her apron crisp even at that late hour. She helped the ladies with their coats, then slipped Gordon's off his shoulders.

A narrow hallway ran the length of the cottage, with both a parlor and a dining room in the front. From curtains to carpets, a dizzying array of floral patterns vied for his attention. Tables were draped in linen and lace, the surfaces cluttered with framed photographs, wax fruit, wooden figures, and other curios. Sprays of larch, holly, and ivy decorated the shelves and paintings, and the smell of freshly cut evergreens hung heavy in the air. His senses were not so much engaged as assaulted.

Alan was nowhere to be seen.

Mrs. Campbell removed a long pin from her hat, smiling at herself in the hallway mirror. "Clara, tell Mrs. Gunn we shall dine at eleven. In the meantime, take our guest up to his room so he might dress for dinner."

As Margaret ascended the staircase a few steps ahead of him, Gordon was haunted by her words: *Christmas is meant to be joyful.* What would make the day joyful for the Campbells? To remember happier seasons before their lives were changed by the careless act of a stranger? Or to have that stranger come forward and offer a long-awaited apology? Gordon was convinced of the latter—not only for his sake, but also for theirs.

Confess your faults. Aye, he would.

When they reached the top of the stair, Margaret disappeared without a word into a room across the hall. Would she seek him out shortly? *Soon,* she'd said. Gordon followed the maidservant into a small bedroom tucked beneath the eaves. The muted colors and simple furnishings were most welcome, and the porcelain washbowl even more so.

"I'll fetch hot water for you straightaway, sir. Is there anything else you'll be needing?"

Aye. He put his traveling bag on a straight-backed chair. *Courage. Strength.*

Before he could answer, she resumed her friendly chatter. "You'll find a shaving mug and soap on the chest of drawers, and the water closet is at the end of the hall. Might I unpack for you? Or press your shirt?"

Gordon opened his bag at once and handed her a fistful of clean but wrinkled linen. "Thank you, Clara." She bobbed a curtsy and was gone, leaving him to manage the rest.

He quickly retrieved his razor and comb, then took a brush to his gray suit coat. Neither worry nor fear would serve him well this night. *Power and love and a sound mind.* Aye, that was what was needed. He'd not find them in his traveling bag, but he knew where to turn nonetheless.

Before long Clara reappeared with a steaming pitcher of water, fresh towels, and his shirt, neatly pressed. "Dinner will be served in a quarter hour, sir."

Gordon bathed, shaved, and dressed, rehearsing the words he intended to say. He would not presume to ask for the Campbells' forgiveness, but he would offer his apology, woefully overdue.

He was straightening his tie when he heard a soft tapping at the door. *Margaret.*

Gordon answered her knock, then fell back a step. Gone were her damp clothes, her soiled coat, her limp black hat. She was wearing an evening dress the precise blue of her eyes and had her sand-colored hair swept into a tidy nest of curls.

It took a moment to collect his wits. "Miss Campbell."

She eyed the staircase before stepping across the threshold. "Forgive me for not addressing you by name." Her voice was low, her mood serious.

He beckoned her further within, catching a whiff of perfume as she brushed by. Not even a bonny lass in blue could dissuade him from revealing his identity. The only question that remained was when.

Standing before him with her hands clasped at her waist,

she said, "I've come to ask you—no, to beg you—to say nothing about the incident at King's Park unless Alan recognizes you. Please?" Her tender voice, her gentle words implored him. "There is little to be gained by opening that door."

"How can you be so certain?" Gordon frowned, trying not to be irritated with her. "Aren't we to confess our sins to one another?"

"You would be confessing my sin as well." Her pale cheeks bloomed like summer roses. "I am the one who told them your surname is Gordon."

Now he understood.

"I could have corrected you then and there," he reminded her, though they both knew he would never have done so in the middle of a crowded railway station. "In any case, you did not lie. My name *is* Gordon."

"So it is." She inched closer. "Please, Gordon."

Her bold use of his Christian name caught him off guard. "But I—"

"Please don't tell them." Her eyes shimmered in the lamplight. "Share our Christmas. Then go your merry way with my family none the wiser. Promise me, Gordon? For my sake?"

He wanted to step away from her, to argue with her, but his feet wouldn't move. "I need to do this…" He swallowed. "Margaret, I will never have another chance like this to make things right."

"But what if it makes things worse?" Her voice was as soft as a child's. "You have apologized to me. Is that not enough?"

"You weren't the one I injured. Not physically, at least." He dared to take her hand. She did not pull away. "I looked at his face that night, Margaret. When you were holding him in your arms, I bent down and saw the anguish in that little boy's eyes."

"I saw it too." A tear spilled down her cheek. "The years have changed him, Gordon, and not for the better. You cannot heal my brother."

"I know." He eased back, releasing her hand. "Let us be agreed, then. If Alan recognizes me, I will tell your family everything and see that none of the blame falls on you."

She looked away as if considering that possibility. "And if Alan doesn't identify you?"

Gordon knew what she wanted him to say. "Then we will enjoy a fine Christmas Eve dinner, and I will leave town on the morning train."

But that was not what Gordon wished for. He'd chosen his words for her family with care and was prepared to say them, even eager to say them. To lay them down like a heavy weight he'd carried long enough. *Cast thy burden upon the* LORD. He should have heeded such wisdom twelve years earlier.

An unseen clock began chiming the hour.

Gordon followed Margaret downstairs, his heart pounding.

Rich aromas wafted up to greet them. However fine Mrs. Gunn's cooking, he could not imagine eating a single bite.

He followed Margaret into the parlor, where a coal fire burned in the grate, an upright piano stood at the ready, and a Norway spruce claimed pride of place by the window. But he'd not come to hear music or see a Christmas tree.

Gordon looked at the young man seated by the fire, his feet planted on the carpet, his back stiff. *Alan.* A lump rose in Gordon's throat. *I did this to you. I did.* He tried to swallow but couldn't. *How can you ever forgive me?*

His carefully planned speech turned to dust in his mouth.

On either side of Alan stood his parents, their posture equally rigid, as if the three of them had posed too long for a portrait.

Mrs. Campbell was smiling.

Mr. Campbell was not. "This is our son, Alan." A faint lift of his brow dared Gordon or anyone else to think ill of his heir. "Alan, meet Mr. Gordon, the gentleman from the train."

Alan offered him a curt nod, nothing more. He had his father's dark hair and eyes, yet he looked nothing like the boy Gordon remembered. His features were hardened, and his brow deeply creased. Not a trace of innocence remained.

Rather than speak down to him, Gordon dropped to one knee, giving Alan a fair chance to recognize him. "I'm honored to speak with you," Gordon told him and meant it.

A spark of anger lit the younger man's eyes. "I can only imagine what our dear Meg has said about me." His voice was laced with sarcasm, and bitterness hung over him like a cloud.

Gordon wanted to say, "I've heard only good things," but that wasn't true. Margaret had made it clear that her brother's company had become burdensome. Instead Gordon told him, "She has related very few details, I'm afraid," to which the lad merely grunted.

One thing was certain: Alan Campbell did not recognize him.

After a moment Gordon stood, trying to shake off his disappointment. He'd wanted more than anything to apologize tonight. But he'd made a promise to Margaret that he would not break.

"Forgive me," Gordon said. "The hour is late, and your dinner has been delayed long enough." He turned to the only person there who truly knew him and offered his arm. "Miss Campbell?"

Chapter Ten

In a drear-nighted December…
About the frozen time.

JOHN KEATS

Even with the fireplace warming her back, Meg felt a marked chill in the dining room.

She eyed her father at the head of the table, then Gordon seated at her elbow, then Alan across from them. The three men had barely spoken, Alan in particular. If he'd looked in her direction, Meg hadn't noticed. What she did see were his dark eyebrows so tightly drawn they appeared knitted together and his frown deeply etched on his face.

Her mother did what she could to brighten the mood by sharing the latest news from up and down Albert Place. Mr.

Dunsmore, the watchmaker, had swallowed a tiny spring that dropped from his pocket into his porridge. An elderly neighbor, the sprightly Mrs. Thomson, had climbed all two hundred forty-six steps of the Wallace Monument on a dare. And Mr. Kirkwood had papered the Stewarts' entire hallway with the floral print upside down.

"Do not think me a gossip," she cautioned Gordon, "for I report only those stories I know to be true."

Gordon assured her, "That is my credo as well, madam."

"Spoken like a true newspaperman," Meg said, thinking to arouse the interest of her father or brother, both avid readers. But neither responded. The presence of a dinner guest had certainly stifled her brother's ire, for which she was grateful. But he might yet recognize Gordon, even if she had not.

The sooner they finished dinner, the sooner everyone could retire, and the risk of discovery would quite literally be put to bed. Gordon had promised to leave on the first train bound for Edinburgh. In a matter of hours, she could take a full breath again.

At last Mrs. Gunn emerged from the kitchen prepared to serve the final dish of the night and receive her due appreciation from the family.

"A fine meal, Mrs. Gunn." Her mother beamed at the cook. "The chestnut soup was especially flavorful."

Mrs. Gunn bobbed her head in thanks, then circled the

table with her tempting plate of sweets—shortbread dusted with sugar and mincemeat tarts with pastry stars on the crust. Clara followed close on her heels, pouring fresh coffee.

"Every course was delicious," Meg told the round-shouldered cook. Mrs. Gunn's silvery hair had escaped from beneath her cap, and her eyes were bleary. *Poor woman.* It was nearly midnight.

When Mrs. Gunn served Alan, he didn't bother to express his gratitude, yet he'd eaten numerous servings of salmon, pork, and pheasant, of turnips, carrots, and potatoes. Gordon, perhaps to make up for her brother's silence, warmly commended Mrs. Gunn, though he'd taken only a few bites of her food.

Too tired to eat, Meg supposed. Or upset over seeing Alan.

Or disappointed that she would not allow him to make a full confession.

Meg took a forkful of mincemeat tart, which now tasted like dry, flavorless crumbs, so acute was her shame. *Forgive me, Gordon.* It was pure selfishness on her part, not wanting to upset her father or enrage her brother. Mr. Shaw had honored his promise, an admirable trait in a man. But she shouldn't have forced him to answer to a name that wasn't his own.

Thou shalt not bear false witness. Aye, she knew the commandment and had broken it soundly. Meg burned her tongue on the coffee, desperate to swallow the bit of crust before she choked.

The moment the last empty cup clinked against its saucer, her father stood, signaling the end of the meal. "I'll see you to your room, Alan."

Gordon rose as well. "Might I be of assistance?"

Meg heard the earnestness in his voice, the desire to do something, anything, to make amends.

Alan quashed his offer at once. "We've no need of your help."

When Gordon resumed his seat, a defeated look on his face, Meg understood. How many times had Alan snapped at her, chopped off her words, ignored her, or made her feel small?

Father pulled Alan's chair away from the table, then helped him stand and move forward with halting steps. Though her brother wore a pronounced frown, his expression seemed more practiced than genuine.

Meg looked down, ashamed of her thoughts. Yet sometimes she wondered if Alan might be more capable than he let on. When she'd lived at home, on two occasions she'd walked past Alan's ground-floor bedroom and spied him standing by the window. She'd said nothing to Alan or to their parents. How could she without seeming heartless? If her brother had discovered some way to stand for a moment on his own, was that not a blessing?

By the time Meg lifted her head, Alan and her father were gone from the room.

Meg sighed into the morning darkness of her cold bedchamber, convinced she could see her breath if the lamp on her bedside table were lit. Even burrowed underneath three woolen blankets, she was shivering. The coals in her fireplace needed to be stirred to life. But her warm slippers were in her trunk. On the train. In a snowdrift.

Daybreak would not come for two hours or more. Yet in homes scattered across Edinburgh's New Town, her students would be well awake by now, curled up by the hearth, waiting for the rest of their households to appear so the day's festivities might commence. Stockings would be emptied into laps and the contents exclaimed over. An orange, round and fragrant. A monkey on a wooden stick. Crayons made of colored wax. A handkerchief printed with a scene from a fairy tale. And deep in the toe of the knitted stocking, a shiny new penny.

Meg sighed, remembering how she and Alan enjoyed their stockings when they were children. She always made him wait his turn while she slowly pulled out her gifts one at a time, cherishing each trinket and toy from Saint Nicholas. Such happy years, when Mum's laughter rang through the house, and Father took young Alan sledding at the King's Knot in the old royal gardens below the castle.

But those days were gone forever.

Throwing back her bedcovers, Meg vowed to make the most of her brief time at home. She poked at the coals until they glowed again, then turned up the nearest lamp and began searching through her chest of drawers for something clean to wear. The striped skirt and blouse she'd worn on the train were still drying by the fire, and last night's blue dress would never do for church.

Meg pulled out a gray flannel day dress she'd not worn since she was twenty. The narrow sleeves were patently out of fashion, but with a bit of pressing, the dress might serve. She spread the skirt across the bed and was hunting for a pair of silk stockings when Clara announced herself with a light tap on the door.

"I heard you up and about, Miss Campbell. Here's your hot water for bathing and a cup of tea." She placed the pitcher on Meg's washstand and the teacup on her bedside table, then gathered up the flannel dress. "I'll not be long," Clara promised and left as quietly as she'd come.

Meg sat on the edge of the bed, sipping her tea, overcome with gratitude. In Edinburgh she had neither a lady's maid nor a live-in servant, only a housekeeper, who came once a week. Piping hot tea delivered to her room? Ironing done by another pair of hands? Those were luxuries indeed.

She'd scrubbed herself clean from head to toe by the time Clara returned with her flannel dress and troubling news. "The trains are not running from Stirling this morn, not in any direction."

Meg peered out the window into the darkened garden behind the house. "I cannot believe it's still snowing."

"Aye, miss."

Her thoughts traveled down the hall to the small guest bedroom. It seemed Gordon Shaw would be with them through church, perhaps even for Christmas dinner. Would Alan see him by the light of day and realize who Gordon was?

A nervous shiver ran down her spine, but she shook it off, refusing to entertain such fears. Nothing to be done but dress for the day and prepare her heart for whatever might come.

"Shall we see if it still fits?" Meg slipped her arms into the separate bodice, with its boned seams and darts, then began fastening the myriad tiny hooks that held the garment together. An endless process, especially with her fingers trembling from the cold.

Clara helped her step into the skirt, then tied the silk sash into a neat bow at her waist. "You look lovely, miss. The light gray suits your coloring."

Meg thought the bodice a bit snug, and one gilt button was missing from her cuff, but she'd not be ashamed when she went downstairs. In a matter of minutes Clara styled her hair, brushing it into a smooth chignon and pinning it at the nape of her neck.

Pleased with the girl's work, Meg caught Clara's eye in the mirror. "I don't suppose I could coax you into going back to Edinburgh with me?"

Clara smiled at the compliment, but Meg knew she would never leave home. Clara's entire family lived in Stirlingshire. For her, the capital was another world, best seen from a distance.

Both women were soon tiptoeing down the stairs, trying not to wake the sleeping household. Clara returned to her duties in the kitchen while Meg stepped into the parlor, where a fire burned brightly, and the lamps gave the room a warm glow.

She breathed in the familiar scent of evergreens and beeswax, then looked up to admire the spruce, which nearly touched the ceiling. The tree was trimmed with garlands of berries, delicate glass ornaments, and small white candles clipped onto the branches. An angel perched on top, brass trumpet in hand.

Around the base of the tree lay a swath of red fabric with a cluster of mysterious packages waiting to be opened. They'd not been there last evening. *Bless you, Mum.* How many Christmas Eves had her mother slipped into the parlor to wrap gifts in brown paper and twine long after the rest of the household lay snug in their beds?

Blinking away tears, Meg knelt by the few gifts she'd placed under the tree the night she'd arrived. None were expensive, yet she'd chosen them with care. As she picked up each one, making certain its tag was still in place, she thought of Gordon spending Christmas morning with strangers and not having a single present with his name on it.

She eyed the two items she'd purchased for her brother, running her fingertip across the rough twine, weighing what might be done. As a boy, Alan would have gladly shared one of his gifts with a child who had none. Did she dare remove the tag and give the present to Gordon instead? She felt guilty even considering the idea, yet it seemed unfair for him not to have even one small gift to open.

Wait. Meg was on her feet in an instant and hurrying up the staircase. *Mr. Forsyth's scarf.* When Meg pulled open the bottom drawer, the strong scent of cedar wafted out. She reached inside, then smiled. *Aye. Still there.* She buried her nose in the soft wool, inhaling the spicy aroma, and held up the scarf to the lamplight for closer examination. The small blocks of cedar, freshly sanded each month, had kept the moths away just as she'd hoped.

Gordon Shaw need not know the history behind his gift. But he did need a scarf.

As Meg stepped into the upstairs hall, she heard a door close. Instinctively, she hid the scarf behind her back and turned toward the sound. "A happy Christmas to you, Mr. Gordon."

"And to you." He started toward her. "Clara tells me there'll be no train to Edinburgh this morning."

Was he disappointed or relieved? Meg couldn't be certain, not by his tone of voice or by his expression. "You are welcome to stay as long as necessary."

"For your family's sake I hope that won't be more than a few hours." Gordon walked closer, his gaze now alight with curiosity as he inclined his head, making an exaggerated effort to see what she was holding out of view. "Do you always rise this early?"

"I do." She pressed her back to the wall. "Especially when I have presents to wrap."

"Oh." He stopped an arm's length away. "I hadn't... That is, I didn't..."

Even in the dim lighting, Meg could see the ruddy color in his cheeks. "Mr. Gordon, you've no need..."

He was already halfway to the guest room. "I'll be down shortly, Miss Campbell."

She watched the door close, his scarf still tucked behind her back.

Chapter Eleven

God looks not to the quantity
of the gift,
but to the quality of the givers.

FRANCIS QUARLES

Gordon scattered the contents of his traveling bag across the guest room bed. What sort of presents could he hope to find among wrinkled clothes and folded newspapers? Nothing of real value, to be sure. Still, the Campbells might appreciate the gesture, especially Margaret. And if his meager offerings served as a silent apology, if his gifts softened their hearts even a little, would that not be a good and godly thing?

He smoothed out Monday's issue of the *Stirling Observer* for wrapping paper and employed his pocketknife to turn one length of twine into four. Then he set aside the few items that showed promise. All were new, purchased in Glasgow before he left. Practical things, useful to a traveling newspaperman.

The neatly rendered map of Stirlingshire might suit a bank clerk's penchant for details. Mrs. Campbell would surely enjoy his small clothbound edition of Queen Victoria's *Leaves from the Journal of Our Life in the Highlands,* which he'd planned to read during his quiet Christmas in Edinburgh.

Alan's present would require the greatest sacrifice, and rightly so—a mahogany fountain pen from a stationer on Argyle Street with twenty leaves of fine writing paper. Of course, whatever the quality, paper and pen were no substitute for a heartfelt apology.

Forgive me, Alan. He would never have the chance to say those words. Not if he honored his promise to Margaret.

Gordon reached for the last present, an item he seldom traveled without—pure white candles. When gaslights failed and lamp oil could not be found, candles saw him through. He rubbed his thumb across the surface of each one, feeling for nicks and dents. An inexpensive gift but well suited for a woman who wanted candles in every window on Christmas Eve.

Would she see only wax and wick? Or might she grasp a deeper meaning? *Light is better than darkness, Margaret, and the truth is better than lies.*

On their long walk through the snowy countryside, when she'd bared her soul to him, Gordon had caught a glimpse of Margaret at fourteen. Vulnerable. Innocent. Fragile. However polished and grown-up her appearance this morning, he still saw a brokenhearted young lass with tears in her eyes.

I'm sorry, Margaret. He not only understood her pain; he shared it many times over.

On a small square of stationery, Gordon wrote out the traditional shopkeepers' blessing, offered whenever tapers were given to customers at yuletide. Then he added a verse that was particularly meaningful to him. He tucked the paper between the candles, rolled up the lot in newspaper, and bound it with twine.

His turn as Saint Nicholas done, Gordon drew a long, slow breath. The aroma of freshly baked bread filled his nostrils. Breakfast would not be long in coming.

Working quickly, he packed his clothes and other belongings so he'd be ready to leave at a moment's notice when the railway reopened. After consulting the mirror over the washstand once more, he collected his packages and slipped downstairs, hoping he could deposit them under the tree without anyone noticing.

But when he turned the corner, there was Margaret, seated beside the parlor window, her gray skirt fanned around her.

Her eyes widened when she saw the packages in his hands.

"Sir, I must assume you've raided the drawers of our guest room."

"A fine idea." He smiled a little and was pleased when she did the same. "As it happens, I'd been carrying your gifts with me all along." He bent to add his presents to the growing pile, then looked up at her. "My traveling bag is packed, Miss Campbell. Rest assured, I'll not overstay my welcome."

Her smile faded. "But you *will* join us for Christmas breakfast?"

"Oh, aye." Had he sounded eager to depart?

"Later we'll walk to church for the carol service."

Gordon looked across the street to the public halls, completed the year he'd left Stirling. The arched windows and rounded stone urns were barely visible through the heavy snowfall. "I thought you might have tramped through enough snow."

"I have indeed." Margaret stood as the mantel clock began to chime the hour. "I've also missed too many worship services of late."

"Then we shall remedy that this morning," he said lightly, not wanting her to feel scolded. He walked with her across the entrance hall and into the dining room, where the family was gathering for breakfast.

Gordon looked at the sparkling table—the polished glasses, the gleaming silver, the flickering candles—and thought of all the twenty-fifths of December he'd spent alone, grieving the loss of his parents and wishing he had a true home. It was all he could do to say, "Happy Christmas."

Mrs. Campbell hurried over, her hands aflutter. "And a happy Christmas to you, Mr. Gordon. Come and break bread with us." She guided him along the sideboard with its array of baked scones and yeast rolls, plump sausages and thick-sliced bacon, boiled hens' eggs and porridge. "Eat your fill, for we'll not dine again until two."

Gordon covered every inch of his plate, hoping no one could hear his stomach growl. When he took his seat, Clara stepped forward to pour his tea. Margaret soon joined him at the table, but Alan's place remained unoccupied.

A brief lull in the conversation followed while knives and forks stayed busy. Finally Mrs. Campbell put her napkin to the side and took up her duties as hostess. "We're fortunate to have Mr. Campbell home with us today and tomorrow," she said, smiling at her husband. "Every year on Boxing Day our family attends the curling matches in King's Park."

Gordon froze, a spoonful of porridge halfway to his mouth.

"That is where our dear Alan was injured years ago," Mrs. Campbell said, her gaze landing on her son's vacant chair. "Even so, he bravely faces those difficult memories."

Gordon slowly put down his spoon. "I see."

Mr. Campbell crooked his finger in Clara's direction,

summoning more tea. "Does that mean you don't agree with our taking him there?"

"N-no, sir." Gordon looked at him. "I would never presume... He is...your son."

"So he is."

Breakfast suddenly lost its appeal. Gordon wanted one thing only: to speak the truth. At once. He turned to Margaret, silently pleading with her. *I must tell them. Now. I must.* He saw the fear in her eyes and knew she understood what he was thinking. *Please, Margaret?*

She shook her head ever so slightly, then mouthed the words *Not yet.*

How much longer did she think he could bear it? Pretending to be someone else. Hiding behind his Christian name. When he pushed aside his plate in determination, Clara whisked it away as if the food had caused some offense.

"I see you've had enough," Mrs. Campbell said cordially. "If you'll not object, we'll open our presents."

Gordon shot to his feet. "Of course, madam." *Gift giving?* How could he possibly sit through the yearly ritual now? The endless shaking of boxes. The careful unwrapping. The feigned surprise when a package that felt like a book was, in fact, a book.

Enough, Gordon. Once he broke his vow to Margaret and told them who he was, the joys of this day would end. Could he not allow them a few happy moments? He waited for the others to rise from the table, then followed them into the parlor, silently exhaling to ease the tension in his body. A half hour, no more, and he would tell them.

Margaret sat on a round piano stool drawn close to the Christmas tree while her mother perched on an upholstered chair with short legs and a fan-shaped back. After a bit Mr. Campbell escorted his son into the parlor from an adjoining room—Alan's bedchamber, by the look of it.

Gordon had to remind himself that Alan was twenty-two. With his stooped posture and shuffling gait, he appeared far older. Once he was seated, Alan brushed back a shock of dark hair from his brow and fixed Gordon with a cold stare.

Take a long look, Alan. Gordon stayed where he was, standing in the doorway, waiting for an opportunity. If Alan named him, the truth would come to light without any broken promises. But he saw no hint of recognition in Alan's dark eyes.

Rather than claim a chair, Gordon moved toward the tree. "May I bring you each a gift?"

Mrs. Campbell clapped her hands together. "You dear man! However did you manage?" She opened her gift at once, tearing away the newspaper like an eager child. "Oh, I've been meaning to read this for many years," she assured him. "Ever since our Margaret was born."

Mr. Campbell showed little emotion when he pulled off

the twine. But appreciation shone in the man's eyes when he unfolded the map. "Very nicely done," he said.

Gordon was glad he'd chosen well yet felt certain the map would be torn to shreds the moment he revealed his name. Had he ever known such a Christmas? When he placed Alan's gifts in his lap, he feared the young man might brush them onto the floor.

"You've no need to shower me with presents," Alan said gruffly.

Was he insulted? Or embarrassed? Gordon said nothing, merely watched as Alan gave the pen a cursory glance and ignored the writing paper altogether. No thanks were offered, for which Gordon was almost relieved, knowing what was to come.

One present remained. "This is for you, Miss Campbell."

She dutifully patted and squeezed the lumpy package. "Is it…hmm." When Margaret finally opened it, she held out her gift for the others to see. "Candles."

"How lovely," her mother said, though her tone was not convincing.

"There's a note," Gordon explained, already sorry he'd given Margaret something so trivial.

She read it aloud, her voice softening with each word. "A fire to warm you by, and a light to guide you."

Gordon nodded. "I believe I wrote something else."

She looked down at the bottom of the paper. "By his light I walked through darkness."

"The words aren't mine." Gordon waited until she looked up, praying she might understand. "Even so, they speak the truth, Miss Campbell. As I must do now."

Chapter Twelve

I am not what I once was.

HORACE

Gordon implored her with his eyes, with his heart. *Please, Margaret. I must tell them the truth.*

"No," she moaned. The candles spilled from her lap.

He quickly retrieved them, leaning as close to her as he dared. "I beg of you, Miss Campbell. Twelve years is long enough."

"Long enough for what?" Alan asked sharply.

"The gentleman was not speaking to you, dearest," said Mrs. Campbell, her tone kind but firm.

Gordon placed the candles back in Margaret's lap, then

lightly rested his hand on hers, longer than was proper. He merely wanted to comfort her, to assure her that he would take all the blame upon himself.

Then he straightened and faced the others, praying for strength far beyond his own. *Fear not, for I am with thee.* The words rang in his heart so loudly they seemed to fill the room.

"I am not who you think I am," he began, turning first to Margaret's parents and then to Alan. "You know me as Mr. Gordon, but that is a half truth."

Mrs. Campbell frowned, a deep crease in her brow. "When Margaret introduced you to us, she said…she…"

"I know." Gordon looked down at her bowed head and the soft knot of hair at the nape of her neck. "*Mr. Gordon* is the name I gave her."

"Out with it then," Mr. Campbell urged. "What is your name, sir?"

Gordon squared his shoulders, preparing for the worst. "I am Gordon Shaw."

A beat of silence followed. And then a roar.

"*You!*" Alan screamed.

"Aye." Gordon faced him squarely. "I am the one who injured you twelve years ago. And I cannot apologize enough—"

"No, you cannot." Alan's countenance was a storm cloud, dark and menacing. "How dare you! How *dare* you come into this house!"

The young man's fury crashed over Gordon like a wave. "I never should..." Gordon swallowed and started again, turning toward Mrs. Campbell, whose look of anguish nearly undid him. "Forgive me, madam. I never should have accepted your hospitality—"

"And yet you did." Mr. Campbell was standing now.

"Sir, I only wanted—"

"You rode in our carriage. You ate at our table. You slept in our guest chamber. And you let our servants do your bidding." The man's voice was low and as taut as a hangman's rope. "You looked at our Alan, our only son, and still you said *nothing*?"

Gordon felt sick. Every word was true. "Indeed, I did all those things." *And I deceived your daughter when first we met.* As her father drew closer, Gordon held his ground, remembering what had brought him to this moment. *Speak forth the words of truth and soberness.*

"I'd had a belly full of whisky that night," Gordon told them. He tasted it still. "I had no business being on the ice, let alone holding a granite curling stone. What I did was foolhardy and utterly wrong. I tried to apologize the next day, but—"

Alan cut him off. "Then or now, your apology changes nothing. I am still in this chair."

Gordon made himself look at the lad. At his face lined with pain. At his broken body. "I never imagined..." *Aye, you did.*

Gordon started again. "That is, I hoped with all my heart that you had recovered from your injury."

Alan's dark eyes narrowed. "As you can see, I did not."

Gordon sighed. "I am sorry for that most of all."

"And yet you came bearing gifts?" Mr. Campbell's face was mottled with red as he gestured toward Gordon's presents, now scattered about the room. "Did you mean to earn our regard and therefore soften the blow when you made your confession?"

"No, I meant…" *The truth, Gordon.* "Aye. Perhaps I did, a little."

The room fell silent, the air as cold as the snow falling outside the parlor window.

After a lengthy pause Mrs. Campbell said in a subdued voice, "Your presents were very nice, Mr. Shaw."

Her husband frowned at her, then said to Gordon, "I turned you away when you came to our door twelve years ago. And I would have turned you away last night had I known who you were."

When Margaret lifted her head, Gordon realized what she was going to say. *I knew who he was.* He saw it in her eyes, saw her mouth begin to form the words. *I knew…*

No, lass. Gordon quickly stepped between Margaret and her parents. "You have every right to be upset—"

"Upset?" Mr. Campbell shook his head. "You underestimate the situation, Mr. Shaw. Nothing you might say or do will repair the damage you've done."

"I know that, sir—"

Alan bellowed, "You know *nothing*!" He leaned forward as if he might leap from his chair if he were able. "Father, shouldn't this man be arrested for his crime?"

"Now, Alan." His mother hastened to his side, her taffeta skirt rustling, her expression tender. "We all agreed, and so did Constable Wilson. What happened that night was an accident. Terrible, regrettable, but still an accident."

Gordon closed his eyes, only for a moment. *God bless you, madam.*

Margaret was standing now, quite close behind him. Near enough he could feel her warm breath on his neck. "Go," she said in a low voice.

Gordon turned and found tears pooling in her blue eyes. "I am sorry, Miss Campbell." *For misleading you. For breaking my promise. For ruining your family's Christmas.* "For everything," he finally said.

Margaret shook her head so faintly he might have imagined it. "Good-bye," she whispered, then stepped back, giving him room.

Go.

Gordon bowed to his hostess, then walked past Mr. Campbell and took the steps up to the guest bedroom two at a time.

Indeed he would go and as quickly as possible. He shoved his arms into his wool overcoat, grabbed his traveling bag, and hurried down the stair, trying to button his coat with one hand. Though his bag was lighter, his heart was not. He had spoken the truth and confessed his sins. But Alan was right. Even an earnest apology had changed nothing, least of all Alan himself.

Gordon caught a glimpse of Margaret standing in the parlor, the candles on the tree twinkling all around her. Perhaps if things were different, the two of them...

No. Impossible even to consider.

He pulled on his tweed cap, wishing again for a scarf to warm his neck. No one stood between him and the front door except Clara, who opened it, then gave him a slight curtsy as he passed by. "Good day to you, Mr.... Good day, sir."

The door closed firmly behind him as the snow welcomed him back into its icy embrace.

Chapter Thirteen

Early impressions are hard
to eradicate from the mind.

Saint Jerome

Through the parlor window Meg watched Gordon struggle to push open the wrought-iron gate against the drifting snow.

Go. A small word, hardly more than a breath, yet it had to be said. Meg knew her brother's temper and wanted to spare Gordon the worst of it. But now that she'd urged him to leave, now that she'd bidden him farewell, Meg felt something inside her crack like ice submerged in hot water.

Gordon Shaw was a changed man. She understood that now. Though he'd revealed who he was to her family, he'd kept his word not to tell of her subterfuge. And when he said, "*Mr. Gordon* is the name I gave her," it was the truth but not the whole truth, withheld for her sake.

Meg knew she should be grateful, even relieved. Instead she was heartsick. *You weren't the only one who deceived my family, Mr. Shaw.* She stared into the snow, a wintry blur of white blowing in every direction. Gordon had already disappeared from view. He was probably bound for the railway station, seeking news. Or headed for the Golden Lion, seeking shelter.

"Meg." Her mother's small hand touched her shoulder. "I wonder…is there something you haven't told me, dear?"

Her breath caught. *She knows.* Meg couldn't bring herself to turn and look at her mother's face. *Mr. Gordon from Glasgow.* Did she think her mother couldn't tell when her own daughter was being less than truthful?

Meg clasped her hands, pressing them against her stomach, hoping to keep her breakfast down. "What…what do you mean, Mum?"

"Mr. Shaw is a handsome man," her mother said softly, "with a keen mind and a good heart. I cannot fault you for being drawn to him."

Meg spun around, her mouth agape. So *this* was what her mother meant. "Surely you don't think… I could never…"

Her smile was bittersweet. "I suppose not, since he is the one who…well…"

Meg glanced toward her brother's empty chair, relieved Father had already escorted him from the room. "I could not do that to Alan," she finally said. "Besides, I have no special attachment to Mr. Shaw. He is a gentleman I met on a train. Nothing more."

"Is that so?" Her mother nodded toward one of the presents under the tree. "I didn't wrap that one. And the tag has his name on it. In your handwriting."

Heat flew to her cheeks. "Aye, well…it's…Christmas."

"Indeed." Her mother reached for the gift wrapped in plain brown paper earlier that morning and picked up another package next to it. "I found something for him too," she admitted. "No one should celebrate the Lord's birth with empty hands."

Meg was touched by her thoughtfulness. "Aye, Mum."

"Find a safe place for these." Her mother deposited the two presents in Meg's arms. "They'll serve no useful purpose now and would infuriate your brother."

Moments later Meg knelt beside her dresser and pulled out the bottom drawer. Once again her knitted scarf had not found a home. The heathery blue would have been a fine complement to Gordon's striking red hair, and the wool would have kept him warm. She'd imagined tying the scarf around his neck and seeing a smile appear above his bearded chin.

Forgive, and ye shall be forgiven. Meg chafed at the gentle reminder. Whom did she need to forgive? *Alan.* The answer came so swiftly Meg could not deny it. Or accept it. Forgive her brother, whose belligerence had driven her from home years ago?

No. Meg shoved the drawer shut, venting her frustration, then marched down the stair. The family was convening in the parlor once more, behaving as if nothing had happened. As if a man had not been swept out the door into the cold, snowy morning like dust on the end of a broom.

Her mother waited by the Christmas tree, holding out her hands. "Come, dearest. We have gifts to open."

Meg paused by the parlor door. *Christmas.* Could she truly celebrate after everything that had happened? She already missed Gordon. Though they'd met a mere twenty-four hours ago, he'd made a deep impression on her, like a thumb pressed into soft clay.

When she looked about the room, Meg realized the presents Gordon had given them were missing. Her mother had no doubt hidden them in the kitchen to be put to good use another day. But Meg was sorry not to have the candles to remember him by, along with his note, a bold scratch of ink across the paper.

By his light I walked through darkness. The loss of his reputation, the death of his parents, the difficulty of starting a new life in Glasgow, with its seven hundred thousand souls—dark days indeed for a man who followed the Lord's leading. Gordon had come to Albert Place seeking forgiveness. Had she extended even a small measure of mercy to him? Had any of them?

Meg reclaimed the piano stool, then inched closer to her brother, vowing to be kind to him, as Gordon had tried to be. She and Alan had cared for each other as children. Perhaps they might be civil to each other for one day.

Alan looked askance at her. "I recognized him, you know. The instant I saw him."

Meg knew better. Had Alan even suspected Gordon's true identity, her brother would have shouted down the rafters. To appease him she said, "There was something familiar about his eyes." *And let that be an end to it, Alan.*

"Christmas," her mother reminded them both, then filled their laps with presents.

The candles on the mantel gleamed, the fragrance of cinnamon filled the air, and for a brief time Meg put aside the many hurtful words that had been spoken in this house and opened her heart to the season.

She unwrapped a pair of lambskin gloves from her father, then a brooch made of tiny seed pearls from her mother, and finally, from Alan, her first snow globe. Even knowing that her mother had chosen it and her father's income had purchased it, Meg still thanked Alan profusely as she upended the lead glass dome, then turned it over to watch the tiny bits of porcelain swirl around a ceramic cottage that looked very much like their own.

"My students will be enchanted with it, as I am," she told her brother, placing it carefully on a nearby end table so everyone might admire it.

By the time the Park Church bell began to peal, their discarded wrapping paper had been added to the fire, the twine was rolled up for another year, and Clara had the parlor set to rights.

Meg slipped her coat over her shoulders, thinking how her brother might brave the snow. "Shall we send Father for your sled, Alan?"

"No," he grumbled. "I have no use for sleds and even less for Christmas carols."

The light faded from their mother's eyes, however briefly. "Very well," she told Alan, patting his shoulder. "Clara will see to your needs while we're gone."

Meg wanted to pinch her brother's ear in passing as she often had when they were young. *Be nice, Alan. It's Christmas, after all.*

On an ordinary day Park Church was only a few minutes from their door. However, this day was anything but ordinary. Meg huddled between her parents as they started toward Dumbarton Road, lifting coats and skirts to plunge their boots in and out of the snow, hailing neighbors along the way.

Jubilant cries of "Happy Christmas!" rang through the air as children of all ages threw themselves into snowdrifts with abandon.

Seeing them, Meg missed her students keenly. In a fortnight she would welcome back a classroom full of boys and girls, all under age twelve. She taught them not only reading, writing, and arithmetic but also grammar, history, and geography. Taxing work, yet she reveled in it and loved the children, however often they tried her patience. Surely by this evening the snow would end, the trains would resume, and she could return to Edinburgh and prepare for the next term.

Though she was content to spend the afternoon with her parents, Gordon Shaw was never far from her mind. Had he found lodging? A warm room? A hot meal? She hated to think of him being alone on Christmas Day.

Meg gazed in the direction of King Street. Was it only last evening they'd walked between the rails together carrying little Tam?

Alas, Gordon had taken her at her word. *Go.*

Chapter Fourteen

The more we know,
the better we forgive.

MADAME DE STAEL

H ave you ever seen so much snow, Father?" Meg eyed
the drifts piled high against the town wall as she
climbed up the steep road leading to the Corn Exchange.

"Aye. The year they finished this church, when you were a
wee girl." He turned toward the Gothic gables and soaring bel-
fry of Park Church. "We had snow over the windowsills and
halfway up the door."

As they neared the broad entrance opposite the town wall,
she looked up at the rose window in the north gable and recalled sitting in the pew each Sunday counting the stained glass

panes that fanned out from the center like a carriage wheel. *I've missed too many worship services of late.* So she'd confessed to Gordon, but the truth was, she'd not been to church in months.

Remember the sabbath day. Meg had not forgotten, but she had been neglectful. She touched the stone around the arched doorway, deciding this was the perfect day to begin anew. *I will remember thy wonders of old.*

"We're in time for the bidding prayer," her mother whispered. They crossed the threshold with due reverence and moved into the sanctuary.

Amid the plastered walls and cast-iron columns, a hundred familiar faces waited. Edith Darroch and Johnny were there. Mr. Dunsmore, the watchmaker, with his plump wife and four roly-poly children claimed an entire pew.

Mrs. Corr made a brief appearance, sitting at the far end of the Campbells' pew before joining her family. Pushing her spectacles into place, she began filling Mum's ear with the latest from Stirling station. Meg picked up every other word. Snowbound trains all up and down the Caledonian line. Their own train still sitting where they'd abandoned it last eve. Mr. McGregor taken ill. No good news from that quarter, then.

Whatever heat the church had to offer was little match for the weather. The parishioners shivered in the pews, coats buttoned to the chin, teeth chattering as they nodded at one another in greeting. When Reverend Duncan bade them pray, a hush fell over the sanctuary, and his petition carried forth, first pew to last.

Meg bowed her head and drew in a quiet breath. The stillness reminded her of standing in the quiet countryside last evening. She listened, eyes closed, as the words fell on her like fresh snow.

"Heavenly Father, we gather to celebrate the birth of your Son, our Savior."

The tension inside her slowly began to unwind. She heard the minister's voice but deeper still, another voice, even more tender. *I have loved thee with an everlasting love.* Tears welled up, threatening to spill onto her lap. Meg knew this voice, these words, their meaning. On any other day she might have resisted his love, knowing herself to be unworthy. But on Christmas morning in a candlelit sanctuary she'd known since childhood, Meg could not refuse him. And did not wish to. *With loving-kindness have I drawn thee.* Her breathing deepened, and a sense of warmth moved through her, despite the frigid temperature.

When Reverend Duncan said, "Amen," Meg lifted her head and her heart as well, prepared to worship the Christ born this day. *I am glad to be here, Lord.*

Lessons were read from Genesis and Isaiah, telling the stories of Adam and the Son of God, of sin and redemption. Carols from centuries past were sung without hymnal or organ, the lyrics pouring forth with all the joy of the season.

Good Christian men, rejoice
With heart, and soul, and voice;
Give ye heed to what we say:
News! News!
Jesus Christ is born to-day.

When the lessons moved to the gospels of Luke, then Matthew, then John, the ancient story came alive once more. A handmaid of the Lord said, "Behold," and Joseph learned there was no room for them in the inn, and the angels sang, "Glory to God in the highest," and the wise men saw the star and rejoiced with exceeding great joy.

Meg was overcome, just as the shepherds and the angels and the wise men had once been. *News! News!* She'd never sung with more conviction.

Hark the herald angels sing,
"Glory to the newborn King!
Peace on earth and mercy mild,
God and sinners reconciled!"

After the last note had rung out and the congregation had begun moving toward the door, the words of the carol prodded at Meg—two in particular, and rather sharply. *Peace. Mercy.*

She frowned as Alan came to mind again. *Ye ought rather to forgive him, and comfort him.* Even if he didn't offer peace to anyone around him? Even if he didn't ask for mercy? *Aye, even then.*

When the door of the church swung open, Meg looked up to find the snowfall had stopped. The wind too. A faint wash of sunlight shone in the pale gray sky.

"Will you look at that?" Mrs. Corr exclaimed, tipping back her head to take it all in. Her hat promptly fell off and landed in the snow. Within seconds her children ran off with her brown felt bonnet, squealing and tossing it in the air. "Now look what I've done." She started after them, then called over her shoulder, "Mr. Corr is at the railway station. I'll send word when the trains are running." She nodded at Meg. "I know you are eager to return to Edinburgh."

Meg saw the disappointment on her mother's face. Would another day at home be so difficult? "I plan to remain in Stirling through Boxing Day," Meg announced, surprising herself and her parents as well.

Her mother was smiling once more. "You've been most helpful, Mrs. Corr." She linked arms with her husband and with Meg. "We'd best go. Alan will be anxious to see us."

As they slipped and slid their way home, Meg turned over in her mind what she might do or say to mend things with her brother. *I care for you.* Aye, that was the most important thing he needed to hear. If she pictured Alan at ten—happy, laughing, carefree—those words would come more easily.

Clara welcomed them home with a pot of hot tea. "Mrs. Gunn is preparing dinner for two o'clock."

Meg looked down at her gray flannel bodice with its many tiny pleats and lifted the watch pinned there. *Almost noon.* Time enough to sit down with Alan and talk things through. If he had no response—or a bitter one—she would take refuge in her bedroom until dinner was served.

When her father started up the stairs, Meg caught her mother by the elbow and pulled her aside, taking advantage of the quiet entrance hall. In a low voice she explained, "Mum, I must speak with Alan before dinner. We've been estranged for too many years."

Her mother clasped her hands, a tender expression on her face. "I have long wished for the two of you to be reconciled. Meet your brother in the parlor, and I'll see that you're not disturbed."

Meg paused by the hallway mirror to pat her hair into place and pinch a bit of color into her cheeks. Then she smoothed her damp hands across her skirt and walked into the parlor. Though it was empty at the moment, she could hear her father in the next room helping Alan stand, assuring her brother he had a firm grip on him.

Since visits from Alan's few friends had dwindled over the years, her brother often spent most of the day in his bedchamber, which adjoined the parlor and was situated across from the kitchen. It was a large room fitted with low shelves he could reach without assistance. Alan filled them with stacks of playing cards, wooden figures he'd whittled from fir or pine, chess and backgammon boards, and all the mechanical gadgets and curious trinkets Father could bring home for him.

When the adjoining door opened, Alan had a wary look on his face. "You wish to speak with me?"

"I do." Meg exchanged glances with her father. She saw hope in his eyes and apprehension as well. He seated Alan in the most comfortable chair, then drew another close to it, meant for her. She waited until he closed the door before she sat across from Alan. Only the small end table, perched on its spindly legs, stood between them.

"I am so pleased with your Christmas gift," she began, lifting her glass snow globe and watching the particles drift onto the miniature cottage.

Alan's gaze was even, his voice flat. "Mum thought you would like it."

Meg nodded absently, at a loss where to begin. She could hardly say, "I forgive you for being difficult." Alan would rightly be offended. Then she remembered what she most wanted him to hear. "Alan, you must know I care for you. Very much."

He scoffed, "Is that why you summoned me here? To tell me that?"

"As a matter of fact—" She stopped before the scolding tone of a teacher crept into her voice. *Love one another. Aye, only love.* Perhaps if she confessed some mistake or shortcoming of her own and asked his forgiveness, her honesty would demonstrate how much she cared for him.

Meg moistened her parched lips and considered the various flaws in her character and the many errors she'd made of late, searching for one that would matter to Alan.

Mr. Gordon of Glasgow. Her spine stiffened. *No, no.* She couldn't possibly tell Alan that. He would never forgive her. But her conscience would not be silenced. *Alan is the one you wronged most.*

No! If she told her brother, the whole household would soon know that she'd blatantly lied to them, allowing the one man to cross their threshold whom none of them wanted to see. *Please.* Meg was finding it hard to breathe, so tight was her chest. *Please, I cannot.*

Alan was leaning toward her now, indifference giving way to mild concern. "Meg, are you all right?"

"No." Meg hid her face in her hands. "Alan…" She didn't know where to start, how to explain. "I'm…so sorry."

"Sorry for what?" He sounded more like himself now.

She lowered her hands, knowing she must look him in the

eyes and speak the truth. "Alan, when Gordon Shaw came home with us from the railway station, I knew who he was."

Her brother's dark eyes turned to pinpricks. "You knew? And said nothing?"

"Aye...no." She eased back in her chair, putting some distance between them. "I called him Mr. Gordon at the railway station, trying to stop him from coming here." How foolish that sounded! She held out her palms, a silent plea for mercy. "Don't you see—"

Alan banged the end table with his fist. "You *knew*?"

"I did," she whispered. "I never dreamed that Mum would invite him to come home with us. That you would meet him—"

"*Meet* him? I *took a gift* from that man!" Alan shouted, every word laced with pain.

She reached toward him, thinking only of the little brother who once lay across her lap. "Oh, Alan, Alan, I'm so sorry—"

"Stay away from me!" He thrust out his arm to block her, then grabbed the edge of the small table and flung it across the floor, sending everything flying.

"Alan, *no*!" Meg covered her face as a cluster of porcelain figures crashed against the wall and landed in pieces.

The silence that followed was even more frightening. Meg looked down in time to see the remains of her snow globe roll to her feet. The black ceramic base was crushed, the seal broken. A pool of water was seeping into the carpet.

Meg began to weep. "Alan, what have you done?"

Their mother burst into the parlor. "Whatever is going on? I heard…" Her eyes darted around the room, widening. "Alan, you did not… You cannot have done this on purpose."

He jabbed his finger at Meg. "*She* is the one you should be angry with. She knew who Gordon Shaw was all along."

"Mother…" Meg stood with trembling knees, wanting to go to her, to hold her hand, to apologize, but the floor between them was littered with debris.

"She lied to you," Alan snarled. "To me. To all of us."

The rest of the household stood in the doorway now, their expressions as shattered as her mother's cherished figurines.

Her father spoke, his voice calm, distant. "Margaret, is this true? Did you deliberately mislead us?"

She sank back into the chair. "I did. I did. And I cannot even remember why."

No one spoke. No one moved.

Finally Mrs. Gunn said meekly, "Will you be having dinner at two then?"

Meg watched through dull eyes as her mother turned to her servants and shook her head. "Go home, Mrs. Gunn. And you as well, Clara. Spend Christmas with your families. Perhaps tomorrow we will enjoy your fine feast. But not today."

Chapter Fifteen

A good conscience is a
continual Christmas.

BENJAMIN FRANKLIN

G ordon poked at the limp slice of mutton on his plate, then dissected the lukewarm potatoes. Food, aye, and served on Christmas but nothing like a true Christmas dinner.

He glanced toward the inn's windows facing King Street, now black with night. At least the snowfall had stopped, which boded well for stranded travelers like him, hoping to catch an early morning train to Edinburgh.

From across the Golden Lion's dining room, a male voice boomed, "If you're not Gordon Shaw, I'll toss my hat in the cook's broth and call it supper." A moment later a middle-aged man, easily Gordon's height and half again his weight, strode up to the table and dropped into the vacant seat opposite him.

Gordon blinked at him in astonishment. "Sir, have we met?"

"We have, though you were too young to remember." The fellow thrust out his hand. "Archibald Elder." He dispatched a waiter to fetch a plate of soup, then tucked a napkin in his shirt.

The stubble on his chin and the frayed edges of his clothing pointed to an unmarried man leading a frugal life, without wife or valet to look after his grooming. Permanent ink stains on the man's fingertips marked him as a printer by trade, and he sounded like a Son of the Rock, raised in Stirling. Still, Gordon couldn't place him.

"How is it you know me, Mr. Elder?" he finally asked.

The man's jovial expression grew more sober. "You are the spitting image of your father."

Stunned, Gordon put down his fork. "You knew Ronald Shaw?"

"I did, God rest his soul." Archibald leaned forward, his bald pate shining in the lamplight. "You were a wee lad when Ronald and I started working together in the printing shop at the *Stirling Observer*. Exceedingly fond of you, he was. Took you everywhere he went."

Gordon swallowed. "Aye, he did." Vivid memories, long

held at bay, washed over him. Going to his first lantern slide show with his father. Sharing a sack of candied orange peel from the confectioner's. Visiting the Corn Exchange together on a busy fair day. "When did you last see him?"

"Two months before he died." Archibald straightened in his chair as the waiter delivered an aromatic plate of cock-a-leekie soup. "I had business in Carlisle and happened upon him on the street. You were all he talked about, Gordon."

"Oh?" His stomach began to churn.

"Ronald told me you were living in Glasgow and had made something of yourself." Archibald picked up his spoon. "Your father was mighty proud of you."

Gordon couldn't believe what he was hearing. *Proud? Of a son who'd fled in shame?*

Archibald started on his soup, his spoon moving in a circular motion, plate to lip to plate. Between mouthfuls, he said, "He kept all your letters. Knew about your university studies. About your position at the *Herald*. Said you were a fine writer."

Gordon could bear it no longer. "But my parents left Stirling because of something I did."

His dinner companion's face reflected utter confusion. "Is that what they told you?"

Gordon shrugged, wishing he'd not mentioned it. "They never confessed it in so many words, but—"

"Well, I know the truth of it." Archibald jabbed the air with his empty spoon. "Your father lost his position at the *Observer.* Not because of anything you did. Or anything he did either."

The news struck a blow Gordon could not deflect. "How is that possible? No one worked harder than my father."

"Mr. Jamieson, the owner, hired one of his cousins, which put your father on the street without any means of supporting his family. He was ashamed, but not on your account."

Gordon shook his head, trying to take it all in. "By then I'd left for Glasgow."

"Aye, I suppose you had, after that unfortunate incident with the Campbell boy. When your father found work in Carlisle, off to England he went and your mother with him."

Gordon sank back in his chair, dumbfounded. "I never asked them why they moved. I just assumed... I thought..."

"*Och.*" Archibald pushed aside his soup. "Your father didn't want to worry you. He knew you had enough troubles of your own." His mouth broadened into a smile. "Looks to me like you've put them well behind you."

Not as far back as you might think, Mr. Elder.

"Has the Lord blessed you with a wife? A wee bairn or two?"

Gordon shook his head, the skin beneath his shirt collar growing warm. "The newspaper trade can be hard on a marriage. Long hours. Frequent travel. In Glasgow I've four rooms in a lodging house. Most ladies would think it confining."

"Not a lady who loves you." Archibald fished out a handful of coins for his dinner and plunked them on the table. "When the right one comes along, all those fine reasons not to marry will go straight up the chimney." He stood, then pulled a woolen cap over his bald head. "A happy Christmas to you, lad."

With that, Archibald Elder took his leave, departing as unexpectedly as he'd come.

Gordon was still watching his retreating form when the waiter reappeared. "Will you be having anything else, sir? The cook made a fine plum pudding."

Gordon declined, then reached for his money.

"No need, sir." The waiter held out the coins Archibald had set by his plate. "He left enough for both of your meals. Generous fellow, eh?"

"Aye." *But not half so generous as my father.*

Gordon squinted at his pocket watch, lit by a single oil lamp on the low dresser, and willed the slender hands to move. *Five minutes after five.* The morning train for Edinburgh would not depart for another two hours. And the sun would not show her wintry face for two hours beyond that.

Seated on the edge of the bed, he dragged a weary hand across his beard. He'd slept poorly, though not from his tasteless meal or a lumpy mattress. Rather, his mind was spinning, thinking of all that Archibald Elder had told him. *Your father was proud of you.* The cadence of Archibald's voice when he said it and the honest expression on the man's craggy face would be etched in Gordon's memory forever.

Clearly, he'd not crossed paths with Archibald Elder by chance. *Man's goings are of the LORD.* Last evening's conversation was a gift from the Almighty—and on Christmas of all days. No present wrapped in paper and twine would ever match it.

Gordon exhaled into the shadowy room, thinking of another gift—the one Margaret Campbell had placed under her family's tree. Merely a polite gesture? Or was it something more? He'd seen the flat package with his name on the tag and a smaller one next to it, addressed by a flowery hand. Her mother's, Gordon had guessed.

Would he never see the Campbells again? Never see Margaret again?

He'd known her for all of a day, yet he could not stop thinking about her. Aye, she was bonny, but her appeal went far deeper than those blue eyes of hers. She had a fine intellect and a broad streak of independence that matched his own. Margaret also was not afraid to speak her mind. *Go.* She'd made her wishes clear, if not her feelings.

Still, she'd wrapped a gift for him. He'd not soon forget that.

Ronald Shaw had also given him many gifts, Gordon reminded himself. His father had blessed him with his name, his earthly possessions, and his money. Gordon reached into his traveling bag for several pieces of unopened mail, including his statement from the Royal Bank, which showed the balance of his inheritance, untouched since the day he'd received it.

He unfolded the paper and considered the sum. *What would you have me do with it, Father?* The question was not directed at a man buried in Carlisle but at his heavenly Father, whose answer was immediate and undeniable. *He that giveth, let him do it with simplicity.*

Gordon stood and began to pace in front of the window as if gazing at the dark sky might prompt the sun to rise earlier. The banks would be closed on Boxing Day, but the shops in town would be open and bustling by ten—the same time he imagined the Campbells would start for King's Park. By then the curling pond would be crowded with players and ringed with spectators eager to make the most of the few daylight hours.

Go. This time it wasn't Margaret urging him out the door but a stronger, more insistent voice. *Go.*

His chest tightened. The Campbells would not be expecting him—Margaret least of all. And though he'd visited King's Park many times in his imagination, he'd not been there since the accident. Dare he make an appearance at the start of the curling matches? And offer Alan his long-neglected inheritance as a means of restitution?

I would have you be proud of me still, Father.

Gordon paused by the window, his breath steaming the icy panes. Aye, he would do it. He would tarry at the inn through breakfast, then arrange to take a later train to Edinburgh and leave his traveling bag with the booking clerk. The walk to King's Park would require little more than a half hour. Once there, Gordon decided, he would seek out Alan—

No. Margaret first. Lest she think he was trying to buy her affection or her parents' approval with this gift for her brother, he would take Margaret aside and bid her farewell. Better to close that door gently than to bang it shut.

But is that what you mean to say to her, Shaw? Good-bye?

Chapter Sixteen

Who listens once will listen twice;
Her heart, be sure, is not of ice.

GEORGE GORDON, LORD BYRON

Meg stood alone near the frozen edge of the curling pond, absently watching the men sweep the surface with their brooms in preparation for the first match. The air was dry and still but bitterly cold. Before leaving the house, she'd wrapped her head and neck in every woolen scarf she could find—save a heathery blue one in the bottom of her dresser.

If she appeared less than fashionable, what did it matter? Gordon was almost certainly in Edinburgh by now. She could hardly fault him for honoring her request. *Go.*

Meg's throat tightened. Gordon Shaw hadn't ruined their Christmas. She had. Though she'd apologized repeatedly, nothing could alter the fact that she had lied to the people she loved most.

Forgive me. She'd said it over and over and meant it sincerely, yet her words could not undo her thoughtless actions. Her mother was sympathetic but still hurting. Her father's quiet disappointment was even harder to bear. Alan, however, made her suffer the most.

"What kind of sister are you?" he'd growled. "How dare you say that you care for me after doing such a heinous thing?"

When their words and tears were spent, the Campbells had retreated to nurse their wounds. Father had gone for a long walk, and her brother had hidden in his bedroom, while Mum had spent the afternoon in the kitchen, putting away their uneaten Christmas dinner.

With Clara gone, Meg had straightened the parlor on her own. She'd picked up the bits of porcelain and swept the floor, then knelt on the carpet to press a linen towel into the damp spot left by her broken globe. As she'd worked, she'd sought forgiveness from the One who never failed to offer it. *His mercy endureth for ever.*

When the family had reconvened well past sunset, they had dined on cold mutton in silence and sought their beds early. Mrs. Gunn had returned in the morning to cook their breakfast, though much of it remained untouched on the sideboard. Perhaps after the curling match they might regain sufficient appetites to enjoy their belated Christmas dinner, though Meg could not imagine it.

She looked at her family, who'd joined the line of spectators gathered near the tee—a circular area on the ice where each curler would soon attempt to place his stone. Alan was seated between her parents in a light wooden chair they'd brought for his comfort. As frigid as it was, she doubted the Campbells would remain at King's Park more than an hour or two. Soon after dinner Meg would leave for Edinburgh and pray never to have another Christmas like this one.

When the men on the ice began shaking hands and wishing one another "Good curling," a hush fell over the crowd.

Meg inched a bit closer. The effortless movements of a seasoned curler never failed to steal her breath. She watched as the first man lowered his right knee toward the sheet of ice to begin his delivery. Holding a long-handled straw broom in his left hand for balance, he thrust his granite curling stone forward, then glided across the ice, his stone leading the way. Slowly, gracefully, he released the handle and rose, his attention glued to the rotating stone. Time would tell whether he'd given the stone a proper turn of the wrist.

As the stone continued to travel down the ice, two players on his side kept pace with it, using their brooms to sweep the path clear, allowing the stone to travel farther. Their skip called out instructions from the far end of the tee while the granite roared across the ice, untouched. When the stone came to a stop barely within the outermost circle of the tee, the crowd offered halfhearted praise and waited for the next man's delivery.

Feeling the need to defend him, Meg lifted her voice above the din. "He showed fine form."

"Aye, he did, Miss Campbell," a gentleman behind her agreed.

Gordon. She spun around to greet him, her heart swelling. "You're still here, Mr. Shaw. I'm so glad." *So very glad.*

Gordon's nose and cheeks were red from the cold, yet his brown eyes were as warm as ever. He smiled down at her, holding his finger to his lips, then motioned for her to follow him.

Meg did so without hesitation. Joy and fear and anticipation all welled up inside her. She tried to tamp down her feelings, to think and act like a woman of twenty-six. But the lass of sixteen who'd always longed for a suitor insisted on having her way.

You stayed for my sake, Gordon. You stayed for me.

Though he did not take her hand, Gordon remained close by her side as they tramped across the uneven ground, heading toward a copse of evergreens draped in snow. They soon reached the edge of the crowd, choosing a place where they might be easily seen, for propriety's sake, yet not overheard.

They turned to each other at last, their breaths mingling in the frosty air. For a moment Meg thought Gordon might kiss her, so intently was his gaze trained on her mouth. She prayed he wouldn't. She hoped he would.

Gordon slowly lifted his eyes until they met hers. "I came to say good-bye and find I cannot."

His words hung in the gray morning stillness, warming her.

After a long silence Meg confessed, "When you left yesterday... When my father sent you away..." She looked down, embarrassed to be speaking so freely. But it had to be said. "I couldn't bear to think of never seeing you again."

"We understand each other then." Gordon touched her chin, tilting it upward. "I also owe you an apology, Margaret, for breaking my promise to you on Christmas."

The sincerity in his voice, the honesty in his expression convicted her afresh. "I should not have asked you to lie, to hide your identity...to sin. If you'll forgive me as well, Gordon, we needn't speak of it again."

In response, he gently took her hands in his. Meg felt her entire body relax as if she'd come home from a long day of teaching and fallen into the softest upholstered chair in her house.

Gordon's laughter, low and warm, took her by surprise. "I have never seen you look so peaceful," he admitted.

She smiled. "And I have never heard you laugh."

Out of the corner of her eye, she noticed several people

looking at them. Meg stepped back, suddenly aware of how close they were standing. And how long she'd been gone. "Forgive me, Gordon. I would gladly stand here with you for hours, but my family will be wondering where I am."

He nodded. "I've come to speak with them as well."

Meg began to cool from the inside out. "There is nothing else to say."

"Oh but there is." He tugged his sleeves into place, then smoothed the collar of his overcoat. "Margaret, if we—"

"Meg," she told him. "That is what my friends call me."

When he looked down at her, the twinkle in his eye was gone. "I hope to be more than a friend to you, Meg. But if your parents and Alan will not allow me in their home, we cannot hope for such a future."

"I am an adult, and so are you," she reminded him. "We do not need their permission—"

"No, but we do need their blessing," Gordon said firmly. "More to the point, I wish to bless Alan in some tangible way." He took a step toward the crowd, now cheering for the men on the ice. "You said so yourself, Meg. I ruined your brother's life. Let me go to him and see what can be done to repair it."

When Gordon offered his arm, Meg took it, then struggled to keep up, his stride far longer than hers. Her thoughts, however, raced ahead of them both, desperate to be heard. *Please, Gordon. Alan will not wish to speak with you. Please!*

Chapter Seventeen

That is the bitterest of all—
to wear the yoke of our
own wrong-doing.

George Eliot

G ordon slowed his steps, realizing he was walking too briskly for Margaret. *Meg.* A simple name for a woman who was anything but simple.

He'd not come to King's Park to win her heart, but it seemed he had. Or had she won his? Gordon knew only that when he saw the light of hope shining in her clear blue eyes, he'd wanted to kiss her. Rather desperately. Somehow he'd managed to keep his wits about him, but the impulse was undeniable.

Meg. He hoped she would approve of what he was about to do.

As they approached the curling pond, he spotted the Campbells in the crowd. Should he greet them with Meg on his arm? Or might that upset them and derail his efforts to help Alan?

Gordon inclined his head toward hers and asked in a low voice, "Do you wish your family to know of our mutual…ah, interest?"

Meg withdrew her hand at once. "Not yet," she said.

She seemed cooler toward him now. Had he misspoken? Made a false assumption? He didn't know her well enough yet to be certain. But he would know her intentions and soon.

As they drew closer to the ice, to the scene of his crime, Gordon's memories of that dreadful January day grew sharper. Little had changed in a dozen years. Not the narrow sheet of ice, or the circular rings of the tee, or the fir trees surrounding the pond, or the milky gray sky.

He picked out the exact spot where he'd careened onto the ice with his curling stone. *Over there.* And the place where a dark-haired lad had dashed into his path. *Right there.* Judging by the mist in her eyes, Meg was looking at them too. Remembering, grieving, as he was.

Gordon touched his fingertips to the small of her back. "I must speak to your family now. Will you come with me?"

They edged their way through the crowd. Several times Gordon started to take her hand, then recalled her words. *Not yet.* The curlers on the ice were well in view now. He recognized some of them. Willie Anderson, with his long arms and loping gait, and George Hardie, who moved with surprising ease for his age.

Three days ago Gordon had carefully avoided seeing anyone he knew in Stirling. Now he hoped people would look his way and see what he was: a changed man. *I will trust, and not be afraid.* He would repeat that truth in his mind and heart until the words took root.

Meg's parents and brother were directly in front of them now. Gordon squared his shoulders, then breathed a prayer before he spoke. "Alan?"

The young man turned just enough to catch a glimpse of him. "I thought you were long gone to Edinburgh," he said dismissively.

Seeing the Campbells' grim expressions and the neighbors standing all around them, Gordon suddenly wished he'd gone about this differently. Knocked on their door. Posted a letter. Had a solicitor deliver the news. To speak of such things in a public park seemed ill advised.

But he was here now, by divine leading. *I will trust.* Aye, he would.

Gordon moved closer to Alan and dropped to one knee beside his chair, ignoring the cold seeping through his overcoat. He'd prepared his speech and rehearsed it numerous times that morning. But now that he was here, with the curling pond to his back and Alan frowning at him, Gordon realized his practiced words would never do.

Instead, he spoke from the heart. "Alan, I hope you know how very sorry I am."

"So you keep telling me," the lad muttered, his gaze fixed on some distant spot known only to him.

Gordon looked across the pond, feeling the icy wind nipping at the back of his neck. "I thought it best to seek your forgiveness here at King's Park," he explained. "Where it happened. Where I hurt you." He pulled the bank statement from his breast pocket, then looked up to be certain Mr. Campbell was listening. "My father was not a wealthy man. But what fortune he had was left to me, his only son."

Alan looked at him with something like disgust. "Is this meant to impress me, Mr. Shaw?"

"No, it is meant to bless you." Gordon offered the folded statement with a steady hand.

Alan snatched the paper from him and scanned its contents. Then his dark eyes widened, and for a brief moment his angry expression gave way to pure astonishment. "Surely you don't mean for me to have all this?"

"I do." Gordon stood, wanting to include Alan's family as well. "As you know, Mr. Campbell, the Royal Bank will not open until tomorrow. But arrangements can be made and the full sum deposited in Alan's account. Or yours, if you prefer."

When Mr. Campbell reached for the paper, Alan yanked it away. "No! I am the injured party, Father. The money belongs to me."

"Now, Alan." His mother nimbly slipped the paper from his grasp. "Have you forgotten your father is a banker? He will know what is to be done."

Gordon saw the look on Mrs. Campbell's face when she noticed the amount. "Mr. Shaw! You cannot… This is…far too much…" She gave the paper to her husband with a trembling hand.

Mr. Campbell's reaction was slow in coming, as if he was tempted to accept the offer yet determined to refuse it. Finally he said, "We appreciate your generosity, Mr. Shaw. Truly, it's a noble gesture on your part." He pressed the paper into Gordon's hand. "But our son has no need of your money—"

"Give me that!" Alan roared. Then he leaped to his feet as effortlessly as a red deer in a Highland glen.

"Alan!" his mother and father cried out. In shock. In confusion.

The crowd around them backed away, their eyes riveted to the young man standing defiantly at the edge of the curling pond, where the game had stuttered to a halt. Curling stones skidded across the ice unattended as the players watched from the sidelines, disbelief on their faces.

Gordon slowly folded the statement and slid it into his pocket, though his actions were done by rote, while his mind reeled. *Can it be true, Lord? Alan can stand and move about as easily as I do?*

Mr. Campbell stepped forward, visibly shaking. "How long, Alan? How long have you had the use of your legs?"

When her brother did not respond, Meg said evenly, "Father deserves an answer, Alan. We all do."

Alan glared at her, then began pacing back and forth. Judging by his agility, he hadn't suffered any ill effects from his injury for some time. "What difference does it make how long?"

"A great deal to your family," Mr. Campbell told him. He drew closer, anger and frustration clearly stamped on his features. "Why have you remained in your chair longer than necessary, punishing the people around you, when you could have stood and walked?"

His mother reached out to him, tears streaming down her face. "Can't you tell us why, Alan?"

Meg sighed, her face filled with sorrow. "I think I know the reason." When her brother stopped pacing, Meg rested her hand on his arm. "You have always longed for our parents' undivided attention. Even before your injury."

Alan looked at her, his eyes two black slits. "Then I had what I wanted for twelve years. Didn't I?"

Did you, Alan? Gordon's heart sank, thinking of the boy who'd grown up coddled and spoiled by his well-meaning mother and father yet remained trapped in a prison of his own making.

"It seems I didn't ruin your life after all," Gordon said quietly. "You did, Alan."

"Well, I'm a grown man now, aren't I? Which means I don't need anyone to look after me." Alan stormed off, head bent, hands fisted.

When his mother started to follow him, her husband gently pulled her back. "Let him go, dear. We've said enough for now." Mr. Campbell turned to Gordon as if seeing him for the first time. "Forgive us, Mr. Shaw. For blaming you alone when our son…when he…"

"His injury was entirely my fault, sir," Gordon hastened to say. "I'm only sorry he never truly recovered." Gordon watched Alan's solitary form move across the snow. Twelve years of guilt. Twelve years of shame. *Enough.*

The neighbors who'd watched in stunned silence began moving back to their places as a nearby church bell tolled the noon hour. The day's light was half spent.

"I don't understand," Mrs. Campbell whispered almost to

herself. "Why would Alan have hidden such a thing? What possible benefit could there have been?"

Meg took her mother's hand. "He did not want to grow up."

"Oh, but—"

"Our daughter is right." Mr. Campbell said gruffly. "Alan didn't care for school, had no desire to work, and showed little interest in being independent." He touched Meg's shoulder. "His sister, of course, excelled in all three."

Gordon saw the pride in her father's eyes and had some inkling of what had kept Alan bound to that chair. He could not earn his father's approval, so Alan settled for his father's constant attention, though at a terrible cost.

Uncertain of his place, Gordon took a step backward, thinking to leave the Campbells in peace.

But Meg reached for his sleeve and tugged him closer. "I wonder if we might ask Mr. Shaw to join us for our belated Christmas dinner."

Food was the last thing on Gordon's mind. But if it meant a few more hours with Meg, he would gladly sit at their table.

Mrs. Campbell tried to smile, though it did not reach her eyes. "You are welcome to dine with us."

Gordon looked down at fair-haired young Meg. *Not yet,* she'd told him. In light of all that had happened, perhaps she'd changed her mind. "Are you sure?" he asked her in a low voice.

"Aye," was her only response. Her eyes said the rest.

The voice of an old friend carried across the pond. "It's time you tried the ice again, Shaw."

He turned to find Willie Anderson coming toward him, curling stone in hand. Behind him stood the other players, brooms by their sides, smooth-soled shoes on their feet. Apparently the men had seen and heard enough to know who he was. And what he'd done.

"I've not held a curling stone in a dozen years," Gordon warned them, though he eyed the stone with longing. *The game of all others that most makes men brothers,* or so the song went. Until this moment he'd forgotten how much he'd loved being counted among the knights of the rink. "Are you certain?" he asked.

"We're between ends," Willie told him. "Come, show us how it's done, lad." He held out the stone, an irresistible invitation.

Gordon ignored the pounding in his chest and clasped the handle, still warm from Willie's grip. Aye, he would try. And if he made a fool of himself, so be it.

He gingerly stepped onto the ice, taking a moment to get his footing. Along the snowy banks stood old neighbors and old friends. Strangers too, no doubt curious why a man ill dressed for the occasion had been handed a curling stone. Though he sensed their eyes on him, Gordon's only concern was his delivery. If he might simply place the stone in the general vicinity of the tee, he would be satisfied.

He breathed a plume of steam into the air, then swung the stone behind him—once for practice, once in earnest. As he followed through, bringing the stone forward, he eased onto the ice as if he'd done so only moments earlier instead of a lifetime ago. He glided along, holding his breath. When his momentum began to wane, Gordon turned the handle clockwise, from ten o'clock to twelve, and released the stone to trace a curved line across the ice.

Two sweepers went into action, brushing furiously, as shouts erupted from the crowd. Gordon could do nothing but watch, though it was hard to see with tears in his eyes. He had done it. He had come back to Stirling, to King's Park, and had stepped onto the curling pond a free man. Forgiven.

A cheer rang out as his curling stone eased to a stop near the center of the tee. Willie thumped him on the back good-naturedly. "Not bad, Shaw. Not bad at all."

Chapter Eighteen

I can never close my lips
where I have opened my heart.

CHARLES DICKENS

Meg tried to be ladylike, but the others were cheering so loudly she had to wave her arms just to be seen, if not heard. Gordon simply *must* know how proud she was and not just because of his well-placed curling stone.

She waited on tiptoe while Gordon moved through the crowd, shaking hands and meeting strangers, until finally the hand he clasped was hers.

"Miss Campbell," he said warmly.

Meg loved the way he said her name, as if he'd just taken a bite of something sweet. "Will you escort me home, sir?"

He pretended to be shocked. "Home to Edinburgh? Or home to Albert Place?"

"To Albert Place, of course." They'd not discussed their plans for traveling to the capital. Might they board the late afternoon train together? Meg did not wish to be presumptuous, nor did she care to give Mrs. Darroch all the ingredients for a scandalous rumor. But if Gordon sat across the aisle from her in a second-class carriage, as he had on Christmas Eve, surely no one would object.

Her parents joined them a moment later, their shoulders sagging, their faces lined. Alan had made their morning very difficult indeed. "We should start for home," her mother said, her voice thin with exhaustion. "Mrs. Gunn expects to serve dinner at two."

Meg and Gordon walked on either side of the weary couple as they crossed the snow-covered fields. Her father had hired a horse-drawn sleigh to convey them to the curling pond for Alan's sake—an unnecessary expense, Meg now realized. It was a short distance home on foot—little more than a mile—and the snow on Dumbarton Road was well trampled.

They walked in silence for a few minutes, the air between them charged with regret.

Finally Meg said, "I am sorry Alan kept his recovery well hidden," not knowing how else to begin. She took her father's arm, longing to comfort him. "Did you have any inkling—"

"None," he said.

"None at all," her mother echoed.

Meg wondered if perhaps Clara or Mrs. Gunn might have something to say. Servants were often more observant than their employers.

"It doesn't matter how long Alan has been deceiving us," her father said glumly. "The greater issue is why he would do so."

Gordon cleared his throat. "I realize this is a private matter, but if I may, sir…"

"By all means," her father said with a lift of his hand.

Gordon looked at Margaret, then continued. "I know the names of several doctors in Glasgow who might be consulted. There are remedies to be tried and treatments that might be considered."

Her father sighed heavily. "I am afraid a clerk's salary—"

"Perhaps you've forgotten, Mr. Campbell." Gordon withdrew the bank statement from his coat pocket. "I meant for Alan to have this. Now I see it is clearly needed."

Meg swallowed hard. *Oh, Gordon.* She was the only family member who didn't know the amount. But she'd seen the looks on all their faces and knew it was substantial.

"Mr. Shaw…it's your…inheritance…," her father stammered, coming to a full stop. "We cannot possibly accept it."

Gordon exchanged glances with her. "What if it were a Christmas present? It's not polite to refuse a gift."

Though his tone was light, Meg saw how serious he was. "In years to come, Mr. Shaw, might this not create some hardship for you?"

He shrugged, his expression free from concern. "The Lord has asked me to do this. I can trust him to provide for me as well."

Meg had a great deal to learn about Gordon Shaw, but she knew without a doubt he was a man of strong convictions. Much would be said and done regarding Alan in the days to come. For the moment her parents needed time to rest, to think, and to consider what the days ahead might hold when Alan returned home—*if* Alan returned home.

When at last they arrived at the cottage, Meg peeled off her scarves and stamped the snow off her walking boots. "Come, warm yourself by the fire," she urged Gordon, escorting him into the parlor while her parents dressed for dinner.

Meg stretched out her hands over the rising heat, and Gordon did the same. His were lightly freckled, long and lean, and covered in fine red hair. The hands of an artist whose medium was words.

Gordon's eyes met hers. "Which train will you take to Edinburgh?"

"Not the three twenty-six," she said firmly, "for I hear it is most undependable."

He smiled. "I plan to take the four forty-three."

"As do I." She held his gaze, longing to know what was running through his mind. Would they see each other again? Or would he simply deposit Alan's money in her father's account and return to his life in Glasgow? *We understand each other,* he'd said. She prayed that was true and asked the only question she could without risking her heart. "How long will you be staying in Edinburgh?"

His smile faded. "Less than a day, I'm afraid. After my morning interview I must return to Glasgow, or my editor will find another minion to do his bidding."

Meg looked down lest he see her dismay. *So soon?*

Her mother called to them from the parlor door. "Mrs. Gunn is ready for us."

"I'll not be long," Meg promised, then hurried to her bedchamber, needing a moment alone. She quickly bathed her hands and face, then added a sprinkle of perfume before pausing to lift up a silent prayer. *If Gordon is to be mine someday, Lord, please give me patience. And if he is not...oh, if he is not, then give me comfort.*

When she lifted her head, her gaze fell on her tall dresser. *Gordon's present.* She could at least send him home to Glasgow with something to keep him warm.

He was waiting for her in the dining room, his clothing brushed, his hair neatly combed. Gordon spotted the gift in her hands. "Christmas...again?"

"Aye." Meg sat so he might do the same, then placed his gift beside his plate. Her parents had already taken their seats. Only Alan's chair remained empty, though the table had been set for him with dishes, sterling, and glassware.

"Indeed, it is Christmas," Meg said, admiring her mother's table decorated with sprigs of holly and berries, gleaming tapers, and cinnamon sticks wrapped in ribbon. On each empty plate was a Christmas cracker, waiting to be pulled apart.

Meg nodded at Gordon's colorful favor. "Yours first, please." They each gripped an end of the paper-wrapped tube and yanked, then laughed when the favor popped open with a wee bang. A small harmonica fell out, along with a printed Christmas sentiment and a wrinkled hat made from red tissue paper.

Gordon smoothed out the hat at once and put it on his head, adopting a serious expression to match. "Your turn, Miss Campbell."

Her cracker was louder than she expected, making her jump. A moment later she was wearing a pointy blue hat. Two more pops at either end of the table and her parents were similarly adorned—a Christmas tradition even in the most sober of households.

"Clara," her mother said, "I believe we are ready for our soup."

A dizzying array of plates and dishes came and went from

kitchen to table. Roasted goose with chestnut stuffing—Gordon's favorite—provided the main course. Her mother ate more than her share of roasted parsnips, and her father enjoyed the sausages in gravy. Meg saved room for the plum pudding with fresh cream, and they each ate a thin slice of Christmas cake, rich with fruit and topped with marzipan.

Without her brother glowering at her across the table and with Gordon by her side, Meg secretly counted this her most peaceful and pleasurable Christmas in recent memory. But she did miss Alan. Whatever had compelled him to pretend he couldn't walk was a mystery best solved by a doctor. But he was still her brother. And she still loved him.

As coffee was being poured, Meg patted Gordon's gift. "Kindly open it, Mr. Shaw. Then we'll make haste to Stirling station."

He tore off the paper—rather eagerly, she thought—and then sat back with a look of astonishment. "However did you know? I've been wishing I had a scarf around my neck since leaving Glasgow. And such a fine scarf too."

Meg warmed at his praise. "I hope it's long enough."

"I would almost say it was made for me." Gordon cocked one eyebrow. "But since you had time neither to shop nor to knit, I can only assume it was made for another man—"

"And he shall remain nameless," Mrs. Campbell said pointedly. "It was made for you, Mr. Shaw. Whether or not Margaret was aware of that when she held the needles in her hands, you can be sure the Almighty knew."

Meg caught her mother's eye, then mouthed the words, *Bless you.*

Gordon stood, thanking her parents with a sincerity of word and expression that Meg found endearing. "Forgive me for leaving so quickly…"

When his voice trailed off, Meg followed his gaze.

Alan waited in the doorway, his hat bunched in his hands, his face chapped and red. Every word he spoke seemed chiseled out of ice. "I have nowhere else to go."

His mother was beside him at once. "This is your home, Alan. You are always welcome here." She ushered him into the dining room, quietly giving instructions to Clara. A wet cloth for his hands and hot soup for his supper were soon produced.

Meg rose to stand beside Gordon, grateful for his strength at such a moment. "I am glad you came back to us, Alan."

He didn't look up, but his spoon paused for a moment. It was enough.

Meg was not surprised by her mother's tender care. But her father's words were a revelation.

"We are glad you are home, Alan. But there is much to be done to regain our trust and restore your good name."

Her brother looked up from his plate, clearly taken aback.

"When you've eaten your fill," Father continued, "we shall

discuss how you might seek gainful employment and so contribute to our household."

Meg wanted to cheer, to applaud, to kiss the cheek of a quiet father who'd suddenly discovered his voice. Where had he found such courage? Such strength? She knew the answer.

Time would not allow even a moment of reflection, as the mantel clock reminded her. Minutes later she was standing at the door with Gordon and her parents, preparing to bid them farewell.

"You will write to me," her mother said, her lower lip trembling.

Meg nodded. "And I will visit as often as I can so I might see how Alan is doing." She looked toward the dining room. "I confess I am more worried about him now than I was when I thought he was still suffering from his injury."

"Aye," her father agreed. "It will be some time before your brother is truly well."

Go to him. Meg felt a tugging deep within her. *Forgive him, and comfort him.*

She excused herself, then slowly walked back into the dining room. Alan sat alone, his head bent, his plate empty. "Alan." Her voice broke. "Alan…I'm so sorry." Meg knelt beside his chair and eased her arms around him. "I wish your life had been different. But it still can be. And with God's help, it will be."

"No one will understand," he said, his voice strained. "No one will ever forgive me."

"I do." Meg pressed her cheek to his shoulder. "I forgive you."

When she lifted her head, Alan looked like a wounded creature, his eyes clouded with pain. She kissed his cheek, then stood, reluctant to leave him in such a state. "Mother and Father will take good care of you. They always have." She smoothed her hand across his matted hair. "I am your sister, Alan, and I will always love you. Never forget that."

When he looked away, she knew he'd heard her.

Gordon appeared at the door. "Pardon me, but the train…"

"Aye." She nodded and followed him out, then bade her parents farewell once more before she and Gordon left for the railway station. By the time they reached Station Road, they were practically running.

The same wavy-haired booking clerk greeted Meg at the window and exchanged her old ticket for a new one.

"Sir, I have a trunk—"

"Aye, you do." He pointed across the office to a familiar black trunk with brass fittings. "I'll have it aboard the four forty-three. Make haste, miss."

Gordon exchanged his ticket as well, retrieved his traveling bag, then escorted her across the platform and onto the train. "I see our seats are spoken for." He nodded toward the front of the carriage where a family had claimed the first two rows.

"No matter," Meg said blithely. She picked a seat in the middle, making sure the one across from it was vacant.

But Gordon sat next to her instead and nudged her toward the window with his shoulder. "An excellent choice."

Oh my. When Meg looked about the carriage, no one seemed the least bit interested in the unmarried couple daring to sit side by side. "You are sure—"

"Very sure, Miss Campbell." He brushed her hand so gently she might not have noticed. Except it was Gordon.

He lowered his head until it touched hers. "Glasgow to Edinburgh is one hour by rail. That's all that will separate us. A minor inconvenience, easily swept aside for the price of a return ticket. Aye?"

"Aye." Meg closed her eyes, overwhelmed. He made everything seem possible. And indeed it was.

Gordon squeezed her hand as if he understood and felt just the same. "In the Highlands they say, 'Christmas without snow is poor fare.'"

"Is that so?" Meg looked up at him. "Then we have enjoyed a rich Christmas indeed."

STIRLING RAILWAY STATION

Author Notes

It was winter; the night was very dark;
the air extraordinary clear and cold,
and sweet with the purity of forests....
For the making of a story
here were fine conditions.

ROBERT LOUIS STEVENSON

L ike many stories, this one began with a book—*World Railways of the Nineteenth Century*—picked up for a song at a used-book shop, then devoured for months until steam came pouring out. How I do love trains! As for the novella's title, a wreath is not only something displayed during the festive season; it's also the Scots word for "a bank or drift of snow." Once I discovered that juicy tidbit, the story quickly took shape.

Of all the years of Victoria's long reign, I chose 1894 because it was exceptionally cold and snowy that December with a twelve-week frost beginning at Christmastide. Two resource books, both published in 1894, proved to be helpful as well: *Murray's Handbook for Travellers in Scotland* and *Mountain, Moor and Loch,* with pen-and-pencil sketches of the West Highland Railway "made on the spot." Love it.

We also lost two significant literary figures in 1894, both mentioned within these pages: Robert Louis Stevenson died on December 3 and Christina Rossetti on December 29. The epigraph here was taken from Stevenson's novel *The Master of Ballantrae,* which Meg briefly read on the train. Christina Rossetti, whose words appear as an epigraph for chapter 3, wrote "In the Bleak Midwinter" in response to a request from *Scribner's Monthly* for a Christmas poem.

To be certain our yuletide celebration in Victorian Scotland was historically accurate, I turned again and again to Marjory Greig's wonderful resource, *The Midwinter Music: A Scottish Anthology for the Festive Season.* If you love that time period as much as I do, the British television production *Bramwell* might be your cup of tea. Set in 1895 London, the series aired on the PBS show *Masterpiece Theatre* a century later and is now available on DVD. The young Dr. Eleanor Bramwell served as a fine role model for our independent-minded Meg Campbell.

It was pure joy to spend a research week in Stirling, Scotland, with my daughter, Lilly, exploring the hilly, crooked streets, snapping photos, watching *Downton Abbey,* and brainstorming about the Campbells of Albert Place. Those handsome sandstone cottages, built in the early years of Victoria's reign, are still standing across from the public halls, which became known as the Albert Halls in 1896.

If you've lived in or visited Stirling, you may be familiar with Allan Park South Church on Dumbarton Road, where Meg and her family worship on Christmas morning. Because we have a character named Alan and the Campbells reside in the adjoining King's Park neighborhood, I chose to shorten the name to Park Church for *A Wreath of Snow.* The church, built in the mid-nineteenth century, is very much a going concern, and the many-paned rose window is indeed glorious.

Many thanks go to Simon Dawdry, a talented artist in Scotland, for reproducing our vintage Stirling Railway Station in pen and ink. And to my New Zealand friend Marlene Dunsmore, a heartfelt hug for sharing a family wedding portrait that perfectly captured our Gordon and Meg and inspired me greatly. Such a handsome couple!

Several editors and encouragers deserve extra kudos for their patience and support: Laura Barker, Carol Bartley, and Sara Fortenberry, your guidance is ever a blessing. My two favorite in-house editors—dear husband, Bill, and our talented son, Matt—kindly put their red pens to the first draft, and my favorite retired Scottish antiquarian bookseller, Benny Gillies, had a go at the second draft.

Naturally, readers like *you* are why I do what I do. I hope you'll visit the special fiction website I've created for you: www .MyScottishHeart.com. And if you'd like free autographed bookplates for any of my novels, simply contact me through my website or by mail:

Liz Curtis Higgs
P.O. Box 43577
Louisville, KY 40253-0577

You'll find my photos of Stirling on Pinterest at www.Pin terest.com/LizCurtisHiggs and on Facebook at www.Facebook .com/MyScottishHeart.

This holy season and always, may your heart overflow with the joy of knowing, loving, and serving the One whose birth we celebrate. Until we meet again—whether in person, online, or across the page—you truly are a blessing!

Scottish Shortbread

Ingredients:

$1/2$ cup confectioners' sugar

$1/2$ cup cornstarch

1 cup all-purpose flour

$3/4$ cup butter, softened

1 tablespoon granulated sugar

Instructions:

Sift confectioners' sugar, cornstarch, and flour together in a bowl. Add softened butter, using your hands to knead the mixture into dough. Wrap dough in plastic wrap, and refrigerate for no longer than 30 minutes.

Press cold dough into the bottom of a greased 8 x 8 pan (round or square; glass is best). Bake at 325° for 30 minutes or until the edges are *very* lightly browned.

Sprinkle granulated sugar across the top. Cool completely, then cut into 8 servings.

At Christmas-tide the open hand
Scatters its bounty o'er sea and land.
And none are left to grieve alone,
For Love is heaven and claims its own.

Margaret Elizabeth Sangster

READERS GUIDE

I love everything that's old—
old friends, old times, old manners, old books.

OLIVER GOLDSMITH

1. With her vocation as a teacher and her town house in
   Edinburgh, our Victorian heroine has clearly embraced
   her independence, yet she feels an obligation to her family in Stirling as well. How do those two very different
   worlds impact the choices that Margaret Campbell
   makes? More than a century later, women are still trying to balance work and home. What tools or methods
   have you found useful in your life to handle the timeless
   challenge of multiple priorities?

2. Gordon Shaw does many things right, yet he is still a
   flawed hero. What are his strengths, and when do you

see them on display? What are his weaknesses, and when do they get in his way? How does the epigraph at the start of chapter 12—"I am not what I once was"—suit Gordon? Ideally, the protagonists of a story will experience some measure of emotional or spiritual growth from first page to last. What growth do you see in Gordon? In Meg? What do you imagine will happen next for them?

3. Though Alan Campbell begins as a secondary character, by the closing chapters everyone's thoughts are centered on him, which would surely please this troubled young man. What emotion does Alan instill in you, and why? Is it pity? Anger? Frustration? If you were Alan's mother, how would you have handled him in the months after his injury? In the years since he became an adult? After the Boxing Day debacle at the curling pond? What steps must Alan take to have a brighter future? Which of those steps might make a difference in your own life?

4. After reading an early draft of *A Wreath of Snow,* author Francine Rivers wisely observed that several of the main characters tell lies because they think a lie is better than the truth. She wrote, "Gordon lied because he feared the truth would bring rejection. Meg lied to protect herself and her family from further pain." Which other charac-

ters lie—to one another or to themselves—and how might they justify their actions? Meg remembers the commandment "Thou shalt not bear false witness" (Exodus 20:16) and is made aware of her wrongdoing. Why are lies so damaging? How do you remain honest with yourself, with others, and with God?

5. Perhaps you, like Oliver Goldsmith in our epigraph here, "love everything that's old" and so find antiques, museums, and old houses are your style. What time periods do you most enjoy exploring through books and films? As it happens, during the year in which our story is set—1894—Thomas Edison had the first public showing of his kinetoscope, used to create moving pictures. What aspects of late Victorian life might you have found enjoyable? And which ones have less appeal? For you, what is the value of learning about "old times, old manners"?

6. The Victorians and Christmas have always made a happy pairing. Queen Victoria's husband, Prince Albert, brought his family's German traditions to Britain, including a decorated Christmas tree displayed at Windsor Castle in 1841. Charles Dickens's classic, *A Christmas Carol,* was published two years later, and the first Christmas cards were printed in 1846. Which Christmas traditions are most meaningful to you? Is your Christmas tree

freshly cut or artificial? Do your ornaments match, or are they a hodgepodge of favorites, collected over the years? What is the merriest moment during the Christmas season for you? And what is often the most solemn and sacred moment?

7. Home can serve both as a refuge and as a testing ground, which the Campbells' cottage on Albert Place certainly was for Meg. How would you define *home*? And how has your changing sense of home over the years defined *you*? What expectations does "going home for the holidays" stir in your heart? When family conflicts arise during the Christmas season, how might your faith in a loving God help you extend "peace on earth and mercy mild" to those around you?

Emotionally Charged. Richly Detailed.
Vividly Told. Historical Fiction from
LIZ CURTIS HIGGS.

| Thorn in My Heart | Fair Is the Rose | Whence Came a Prince |

"Liz Curtis Higgs maps the human heart with indelible ink. An extraordinary trilogy."
—TERESA MEDEIROS, *The New York Times* best-selling author

A Dramatic Story All Her Own

A Heartrending Saga in Two Parts

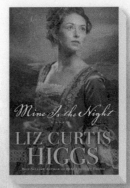

| Grace in Thine Eyes | Here Burns My Candle | Mine Is the Night |

"An absorbing, well-crafted novel with a gut-wrenching plot that will move readers. Highly recommended."
—*Library Journal* STARRED REVIEW

"A compelling tale of love, loss, faith, and forgiveness that is certain to please both inspirational readers and fans of well-crafted historical fiction." —BOOKLIST